More Praise for *Tales with Tails*

"Here is an elegant collection of stories and poems whose broad scope and amazing variety should keep young readers returning to this volume for inspiration and entertainment again and again."

—*Bernette Ford, Publisher*
Color-Bridge Books

"I have a great fondness for folk tales, fables, fairy tales and stories that teach us something about life. *Tales with Tails* is an excellent collection of tales that teach the reader there are many ways to see the world. It is possible to be someone in the world who shows kindness and caring for others. There is also a humorous touch in seeing human frailties exemplified in the natural world. Let's try to see the world from another's perspective, and make it a better place!"

—*Sandra Kennedy Bright*
Library Media Consultant
Director (Emeritus) Office of School Library Services
NYC Department of Education

"These nine tales explore the complexity of relationships between man and animal, and between animal and animal, in habitats and vernaculars both strange and familiar. From the disturbing encounter of man and polar bear to the quiet strength man draws from wolf to bolster his own humanity, the tales invite reflection and discussion on what sets us apart from one another and what binds us together."

—*Claudia H. DeShay, M.L.S., Ph.D.*
Education Librarian
UT Southwestern Medical Center Library
Dallas, Texas

W9-BIB-585

Tales with Tails
by the writers of Pen & Rose

Pen & Rose Press
BROOKLYN, NEW YORK

An imprint of
Harlin Jacque Publications
GARDEN CITY, NEW YORK

Edited by Kiini Ibura Salaam

ISBN-13 978-0-940938-43-4
ISBN-10: 0-940938-43-X
Library of Congress Control Number: 2006900189
First Edition 2006

Pen & Rose Press
www.penandrose.com

An imprint of Harlin Jacque Publications
P.O. Box 336, Garden City, NY 11530
Tel: 516-489-0120 Fax: 516-292-9120

In memory of India DuBois

The Stories

Illustration by Mary Wolos-Fonteno

The Legend of Nookapingwa

by Mary Wolos-Fonteno

THE SUN DIPPED behind a cover of thick clouds at the horizon and Thule sat with her cubs, Tatiq and Qaanaaq, nuzzled against her fur, quietly telling them the story of their ancestor from the North. The story was their favorite and she told it to them over and over since they were born.

"Most of us have never been near the arctic where our ancestors lived," Thule said. "Far north the sun is different; it shines for many months and hides for many months, it's never really high in the sky. The air and the wind are different too. The food is different. Our bellies don't ache from hunger. I have never caught a seal or swum beneath an ice floe." She stopped and thought for a moment, "But that would be fun; would you just love to do that?"

"I would do it all day until the sun went down," said Tatiq.

Qaanaaq agreed, "Especially in the summer when it's a hundred degrees here."

Thule continued, "Polar bears who live far north have a different connection to earth and Spirit, their survival depends on it. But we are lucky too, in a different way. Our lives are not hard, our food is provided for us and we are

Thule	(THOO-lee)
Qaanaaq	(kah-KNOCK)
Tatiq	(tah-TEEK)
Nanuk	(na-NOOK)
The Eskimo word for the polar bear	

3

free to play and contemplate other things in life.

"But no matter where you live," she said, "one thing we all have in common is knowledge of Nookapingwa. You remember, Nookapingwa was the first to have a barrel and every mother tells this story to her cubs when they are young to keep the story alive. It has been so for generations," said Thule. "It is the story of our ancestor—a great white bear who lived in the Arctic."

The cubs listened like it was the first time they had ever heard the story. They never tired of it.

Thule continued, "Nookapingwa lived in the tundra way up in the northern region. They say when he was young, he was powerful, handsome and enormously strong, well over nine feet tall and weighed more than 1,200 pounds after a good winter-feeding. He was a clever and cunning hunter too and his patience helped him to wait hours for just the right moment to dive to the edge of a seal hole, smash the ice and grab a seal. He traveled far and knew every seal hole and every inch of land for miles and was friends with the fox and the owl, but mostly he just lived alone.

"When Nookapingwa got older, men from far south came on an expedition across the northern hemisphere into the Arctic and set up camp near an inlet, somewhere in the western tundra. They sought adventure and looked to conquer the land and catch Nanuk, the great white bear. These men were probably thought of as brave by their race to face such enormous odds against nature, but I think they were just foolish and greedy.

"It was harder for them to exist in the cold than they expected. Their clothes were not suitable for the extreme weather, as they wore no seal or bearskins. And though they felt brave, they were not good hunters and disliked eating seal; the fat was too rich for their stomachs. They had not planned well and didn't anticipate the tundra to be so inhospitable. Early on, they figured they would supplement their food supply by catching fish and animals, and so did not bring enough provisions to sustain them if they did not hunt. After months of rationing their food, their supply barrel ran low. A plan was made to lure a great white bear to kill and eat, and save the skin for a good story to brag about on their return."

"But they never got to do that did they?" said Tatiq.

"No," Thule answered, "they never did."

"Nookapingwa was aware of the men long before he ever saw them. He knew when they arrived. There was a faint almost undetectable scent of them in the air for months that was unfamiliar and of no real interest to him. The wind told him the smell was miles away and besides, he was busy swimming and catching seal. Then one day when the sun was not long in the sky, it started to snow and he awoke hungry. That day he set out to follow the unknown scent. But there was something else he smelled with it. Not seal, but seal meat. He figured it came from another bear's successful hunt, perhaps a mother and her cubs feeding. But oddly, he could not detect another bear's scent along with that of the seal.

"Nookapingwa would go another day following his nose before he reached that smell. What exactly it would be he didn't know, until he came upon a camp, a short distance from the water, which had much movement from snow dogs and men. He had seen men before, but they were Eskimo and he knew what they smelled like. These men were not Eskimo; they smelled different. Concealed against the snowy background, he lay down and blended with the snow observing the camp before approaching it.

"There was much commotion among the dogs which were kept harnessed and tied to prevent them from running toward a bear, should one actually appear. The dogs were alert, they barked and yelped to warn the men; they could smell Nookapingwa.

"Then he saw them—four men. Not all together at once, but individually, then in pairs. They took turns emerging from the shelter to see what the commotion was, but did not see Nookapingwa in the distance. His stillness and camouflage in the snowy landscape had not tipped them to his presence; but the dogs knew. The men were too stupid and arrogant to pay proper attention to the dogs and commanded them to silence. Their voices were unfamiliar to Nookapingwa. But he was not so interested in them as he was in the meat meant to lure him.

"After a while, movement at the camp subsided. His curiosity, hunger, and the smell of fresh seal finally drew him to his feet. The hunters meant the meat only as bait, not a meal, so after eating the meat, which was cleverly tied a distance away from their quarters, Nookapingwa searched for more—that had been just an appetizer for him. By now, the dogs were barking uncontrollably, but could not run and surround him as their instincts told them to do. Nookapingwa's scent and movements made them go wild. The ruckus roused the explorers to the great bear's presence.

"The man who emerged from the shelter had probably imagined he would see Nanuk from a distance at first, and would simply shoot him in a tidy way, taking him down to his death with one clean shot. He would then pay an Eskimo to skin him and would swagger in the glory of the bravery of his kill. But what he saw before him, he could not have prepared himself for. The wind had picked up and swirled snow around the great bear as he raised himself up to his full height and stood before the hunter in complete magnificence. And before the hunter died, he understood the enormity and majesty of Nanuk and the power of his spirit.

"There was surprise on the man's face as Nookapingwa charged toward him. Stumbling, the explorer reeled around searching for his rifle and shouted for his companions to wake up and shoot the blasted thing. The man made wild motions with his arms to regain his balance, and Nookapingwa took it as an invitation to lunch and rushed the foolish explorer with his head down, and his ears back, swiping him with one enormous paw and biting off his head. But not before the man reached his rifle and managed one departing shot, grazing Nookapingwa's right ear. It did not deter the bear in his might. But the ensuing explosions from the guns of the other explorers were deafening and sent Nookapingwa off into the snow, taking the explorer with him to finish him off elsewhere."

"Is that true? Did he really eat that explorer?" asked Tatiq.

"Yes, I believe he did," answered Thule.

"I don't care if it's true or not, it's a good story," said Qaanaaq. "I would have bitten his head off too and eaten the other explorers as well."

"Not me!" said Tatiq, "I would never eat a human. They have no blubber and wouldn't taste good at all and are probably not even connected to Great Spirit anyway."

"All creatures who live on earth are connected to Great Spirit," Thule said gently, "and I think, if you were hungry enough, even you would eat a man."

"So, get to the part when Nookapingwa finds the barrel," the cubs pressed.

"Well..." Thule continued. "The explorers knew there was no hope for their companion, but now they were determined to kill Nookapingwa. Their shooting continued in desperation as the great bear retreated into the snow. The hunters kept firing though they were now shooting into a snow that whipped and stung their faces so that they could no longer take proper aim. They never knew that the last shot actually hit Nookapingwa in the left leg. As far as they were concerned, their expedition had come to a tragic and sudden end. Too afraid to stay any longer, they hitched the dogs to their sleds and fled into a blinding snow that very night, leaving the camp with the empty wooden barrel behind them.

"Nookapingwa's wound from the gunshot was more of an annoyance than anything else. It didn't hinder his movements or his ability to hunt and he was only reminded of it when he attempted to lie on his left side. After some months, the wound healed. The bullet, which was lodged in the fat of his haunch had missed his muscle and bone completely, and stayed in his leg for the rest of his life.

"It would be many months before Nookapingwa came upon that deserted camp again. Spring had arrived and the sun remained longer in the sky. Ice floes started to recede and shift on the water and patches of snow began to melt as the temperature rose. Nookapingwa was heavy from a winter of feeding and scavenged the land on which he had met the explorers. It was then that he found their empty rations barrel.

"Though it no longer held food, a savory smell lingered in the wood and Nookapingwa was determined to open the barrel and investigate. After much rolling and scratching, he finally gave up trying to pry the lid free, for each time he tried, the barrel rolled away, only for him to chase it again. The wood was hard and smooth and slid on the snow like runners on a sled; or it would skitter from beneath him sending him sliding on his backside away from it. He lunged and caught the edge of it with his enormous claws and pulled it toward him, lifting it high into the air, grunting and snuffling, showing his frustration. Then the barrel teetered and rolled right up his forearms and bumped him in the head. Nookapingwa roared and sent the barrel soaring through the air where it landed on a soft patch of melting snow. It spun slowly and came to a stop.

"Despite his annoyance, Nookapingwa could not resist the new thing. He ran toward it sliding on his padded tummy butting the barrel with his head once more, sending it rolling over his back, down his legs and into the water. There, it bobbed and rocked invitingly and Nookapingwa dove in after it, sending it soaring back onto the ice.

"He climbed out of the water and wrestled it again, hugging the barrel, pushing hard with his hind legs while rocking forward. Then it shot from beneath him sliding backward into the water, sending him splayed on his belly in the other direction. He turned and dove into the water right on top of it, pushing off and plunging the barrel downward with his hind feet. For a moment it was gone; he couldn't see it anymore. Then, it shot up right out of the water, and hit Nookapingwa in the chin, knocking him backward.

"The splashing and commotion that went on sent seals swimming in other directions. But for once, it was not seals that Nookapingwa had on his mind—it was conquering the barrel. Again and again he retrieved the barrel from the water only to send it splashing back in. This continued for hours.

"For the next several days, Nookapingwa played with his new toy, forgetting about his hunger. Over and over again the barrel floated, bobbing and dunking him each time he tried to climb aboard. It was the most fun he had ever had.

"Then one of the iron bands circling one end of the barrel bent during a particularly hard pounce from the great bear. The band moved just enough to allow a few wooden slats to slide sideways making the barrel collapse beneath his massive weight.

"Nookapingwa stood up with his front paws raised and let

out several long, low groans and shook his head from side to side. Then he lumbered into the water for a swim. No one knows whether his cries were in victory or in sorrow."

"I bet he was sad," said Tatiq. "That would have made me sad for a long time."

"Me too," said Qaanaaq. "He should have had the barrels we have; they never break."

"No, they don't," said Thule, "but they are not made of wood either."

The cubs were restless and Qaanaaq stood up. He wagged his head from side to side, and let out as low a groan as he could, mimicking Nookapingwa's frustration, then he tackled Tatiq, pretending to bite her. She fought back and they tumbled into a summersault and landed at the edge of their pool.

"Let's find the barrel and pretend we're Nookapingwa," said Qaanaaq.

"OK," she said. Tatiq dove into the cold water and spread her powerful paws as she swam gracefully beneath an imaginary ice floe to the other side of the enormous pool where their barrel lay motionless—but not for long. They played with the barrel for the rest of the day until there was no longer light in the sky.

And so the winter went by much the same as it would for many more years. Qaanaaq and Tatiq grew and eventually stopped needing Thule. She was moved to another zoo, somewhere in Canada, and lived out her years happily in the cooler climate.

Even as they got older, the cubs continued to play with their barrel for years. The crowds at the zoo would delight in watching them, but the bears paid them little or no attention. They had gotten so used to the shapes and movements at the habitat windows, that they no longer seemed to take notice of people watching them and acted as if they were not even there. But of course, the bears could smell them.

They had great fondness for the humans who would interact with them each day, as their scent was the most present and familiar and they responded well to the welcoming voices and soothing tones. But Qaanaaq had to admit that as much as he enjoyed the feeding schedule and their attentive care, given the chance, he still might have tried to eat one himself. Luckily, that chance never came.

Qaanaaq and Tatiq remained together and were eventually moved into a new and larger habitat where another polar bear joined them. After a few years, Tatiq had cubs of her own and passed down the legend of their ancestor, Nookapingwa, to them the same way Thule had passed it down to her and her brother. And so the legend will continue for generations.

Foxes of Fire and Ice

by Debbie Dieneman

ALTHOUGH IT WAS May, a damp chill settled into the air. The rising sun, hidden behind clouds and dense foliage, did nothing to warm the side of the mountain. The newly emerged flowers and bright green leaves were sugared with a coating of frost. Next to tall stands of bamboo and fir and birch lay a path marked by broken twigs and invisible scents. Nothing moved except the snowflakes that began to drift softly down. They covered the early spring buds, and concealed the path and its evidence of life.

Just off the trail, hidden high up in a hollow tree, all was warm and cozy and alive. Deep within a cavity lined with soft leaves, lay a family. Two little noses, filled with the sweet aroma of their mother's milk, nuzzled down for a morning meal. The rare four-ounce babies, eyes still shut, were almost hidden in the fur of rich red-brown and black and white. Wah, a red panda, licked her infants, and they drifted off to sleep again.

The familiar cycle of nursing and sleep was only broken when Wah finally decided she needed something to eat, too. Tiny squeals came from her babies as she moved, but they soon drifted back to sleep again. Somehow she knew that the twins would be safe for a while. After all, she had chosen that tree well.

Poking her raccoon-like face out of the hole, Wah sniffed the air for unfamiliar scents. Satisfied that all was well, she emerged from her den, pulled herself out onto a limb, and looked around. Her bright fur blended into her surroundings, and she was barely noticeable against the red mosses and white lichens growing on the dark bark of the tree. Knowing she didn't have much time, she made her way down the tree head first. Once on the ground, she soon found what she was looking for: a thicket of bamboo. Holding some tender new leaves in her paw, she began chewing. She ate for some time, trying to fill her empty stomach. But her babies came first, and they would be hungry too. Maybe another time she would find a bird's egg or another energy-rich treat. Wah found her hidden tree and quickly climbed back into her den.

Seasons change very slowly on the higher elevations of the Himalayan Mountains. But spring did grow warmer and gradually turned into summer. The air was sweet with the fragrances of wood sorrel and rhododendron. The soft greens of bamboo were joined by the pinks and lavenders of mountain orchids. Everything was growing, including the family in the tree. As the cubs grew, they filled that little nest to overflowing. They were almost three months old now. They rolled and tumbled about the nest as they played with Wah's fat tail. They playfully batted at each other. Full of curiosity, they poked their little black noses out of the nest. Their activity told Wah that it was time to introduce them to the outside world. The big day had come.

Wah waited until dusk, when the fading light made it difficult to be seen. She sat on a branch outside the nest and called to the twins. Mao, the female, was the first to emerge. Excitedly, she practically ran across the branch to her mother. Her twin, Hai, was more timid. He came out slowly, and fearfully inched his way across. But their mother did not worry as she watched him hold on with sharp claws. Wah groomed her children with her rough tongue as they looked around with wide eyes. Then she led the twins down the tree. Mao ran down head first, like her mother. Her brother, true to his personality, went down sideways, slowly digging his claws deep into the bark. Finally they were all on the ground.

The twins looked all around. What an exciting world it was! New smells filled their little noses as they sniffed the leaves, the flowers, and the ground. Some were sweet, but others, like the scent markings of passing animals, made the youngsters recoil. One particularly large pile of scat (left by a passing giant panda), made Hai run to his mother in fear. He hid behind her for a while and stared in the direction of that strange smell. His mother licked his face to reassure him. Soon he and his sister would learn that they were not the only residents in their mountain home.

The sounds were different outside, too. It had been very quiet in their little nest, except for their own squeals and chirps. But in the forest the cubs could hear the rustling of the leaves, the calling of birds, and the distant screech of a macaque. After awhile, they also heard the soft tap, tap, tap of raindrops on high bamboo. The rain seeped in between spaces in the canopy, and soon dripped on their heads. Even though their thick fur kept them dry, Wah took this as a sign to take the twins home. After a clumsy climb, they all snuggled together; safe in their own little den.

From then on, there were daily excursions into the forest surrounding their nest. Mao and Hai soon became familiar with their animal neighbors. Playfully they chased the blood pheasants that bobbed along the trail at twilight. Courageous Mao took the lead, running and pouncing. The frightened birds took off in short flights, scattering feathers and fall leaves as they disappeared into the mist. The twins hid in the underbrush and stared at the tiny musk deer, with their miniature tusks, that passed by in search of food. Occasionally, they caught a glimpse of other small mammals, like shrews and deer mice, scurrying along the trail. They tried to catch them with their thickly furred paws, but the cubs were not quick enough.

Once, a startling horde of golden monkeys swung through the treetops, snapping dead branches and loudly wailing as they swung from tree to tree. Mao and Hai ran to their mother for comfort, who assured them that they had nothing to fear from that noisy bunch. But mother's sensitive nose and watchful eyes were always alert to the danger of larger animals, especially predators like the leopard.

But there was a bigger danger in the forest. Wah did not know that there were often human poachers there, setting traps in the underbrush during the day when her family was asleep. These hunters wanted to catch whatever animals they could; for bones, teeth, organs, and musk could be turned into traditional medicines, and sold for high prices in the valley below. Thick fur could be turned into hats, and striped tails into dust mops, and sold too. But pandas know nothing of this. Once Wah had smelled poachers in the area. She quickly gathered her children together into her den, fearful of those unfamiliar scents. By the next day those smells were gone, soon to be forgotten.

As their world became bigger, so did Mao and Hai. Although they were still cubs, they would soon be as big as their mother. The family moved farther away from their nest each evening, and rarely returned to it to sleep. By watching their mother, the youngsters soon learned to eat the bamboo that would become so important to their survival. They learned to hold it in their forepaws, resting the shoots on a thumb-like wrist bone. But they were still dependent on their mother's milk; for at five months, they were not yet weaned. So after each outing, they found a hidden place among the leaves or high up in a tree, eager to nurse from their mother, and drift to sleep in a heap.

Late one day, as the red panda family moved down the trail, Wah stopped suddenly to sniff the passing breeze. It was winter now, and she was getting more and more restless. Weaning was well underway, and she instinctively knew she should spend less and less time with her offspring. Wah looked at the twins, who were busy sniffing an entrance to a small burrow. Then she quickly turned and ran off through the underbrush. The twins did not notice that she was gone until much later. For the first time ever, they slept without their mother.

A few days later, just after the first snowfall of the season, Wah awoke to strange noises and very strange smells. Climbing down from the branch she had been sleeping on, she crept along, nose snuffling the depressions in the snow. These were unfamiliar footprints, and their scent made her fur stand on end. They reminded her of something, and she knew it wasn't good. Thinking of the safety of her almost forgotten twins, she ran back in the direction she had traveled from a few days earlier. The strange smells got stronger, and she stopped in her tracks, not knowing which way to go. Suddenly, there was a loud crack, and Wah knew nothing more.

That same day, Mao and Hai awoke hungry, as usual. They were still learning to find enough food to satisfy themselves. The twins searched through the patches of snow and dead leaves and became elated when they found a bush of fresh arrow bamboo. They ate together, sitting so close their backs were touching. Without their mother around, they became watchful, too. Ears turned to every noise, and noses were extra sensitive. Survival became the game; play was put aside for now. Late each night, a sleeping place was carefully chosen, and the twins slept fitfully, close together on high branches. They did not know if they would ever see their mother again.

As the weeks went on, the siblings learned to fend for themselves. Even timid Hai became good at leading the way. Each day, they moved farther away from the area that they were born in, as they searched for food.

Winter had brought the snow, but it came with too many brown leaves, and dying stalks. Moving down the mountain now, where winter was milder, they followed the seasonal growth of bamboo. In the lower elevations, the tall umbrella bamboo was still fresh and green. When they found it, the pandas relished in this rare abundance, and chewed each leaf slowly. Each time the twins found another patch of bamboo, or some winter berries, they ate until their stomachs were full.

For months, the two pandas ate, and slept, and traveled. Gradually, brother and sister spent more time eating and looking for food apart, and less time together. After all, red pandas are solitary by nature, and they were getting older. No longer cubs, Mao began to make a twittering, birdlike call as she traveled, and Hai was eager to scent mark everything in sight. Then one day, they each went in a different direction. Neither looked back as they disappeared into the mist of their forest home.

Almost two years later, Wah came back to the area where she had given birth to her litter of twins. She lumbered slowly along the path, for she was pregnant again. Along with her round belly, she sported a black collar with a silver antenna sticking up; fashionable souvenirs from that fateful day when she had been captured by humans. It swayed as she walked, but she did not notice. She was used to the feeling around her neck, and sometimes even forgot the collar was there. She did not know that somewhere it made a blip, blip, blip on a distant computer screen. She did not know that somewhere there was a team of wildlife researchers tracking her every move. She did not know how important she was to the future of the few red pandas left in the wild. She had better things to think about. Wah was looking for a place to build her den; perhaps a hollow tree, or a hidden cave. Back in her mind, she knew there had once been a nest here, somewhere.

AUTHOR'S NOTE:

In their home ranges in the mountains of China, Nepal, Laos, and Myanmar, the once common red pandas are getting harder to find. Habitat loss, deforestation, and poaching have contributed to their decline. And because the red panda's breeding season happens only once a year (and lasts for only about 24 – 48 hours), not many babies are born.

In American zoos, the red panda is part of a captive breeding program, called the Species Survival Plan. Suitable pairs of this highly endangered species are matched up through a kind of "computer dating service." So far, there has been moderate success. But can these zoo born animals ever be introduced into the wild? No one really knows for sure. For now, the future of the "fire fox" is uncertain.

Illustrations by Nancy Rakoczy

Snake's Loose!

by Nancy Rakoczy

That two-headed
monster known as
Larry&Rick
has let
Shshshsheila
out of her cage and
she's S-curved
up splintery cellar stairs
and double S-curved
up scratchy carpet stairs
it's lunchtime
and Shshshsheila's
    deeply hungry

Squivering
slithering
shshshsh-ing
double S-curving
under rugs

double S-curving beneath
kitchen table legs
and double-S'ing
around and around
the kitchen table
heads up family
snake's loose!

Dad's at the table
slurping and burping
up the vinegar black pepper
chili and hot sauce
head cheese his Saturday treat
silent S-curve Shshshsheila
figure eights beneath his chair
to watch and wait for lunch
to come out of its
quivering corner

Lunch has
scampered
scampered
scampered away as
Shshshsheila
double flicks her tongue
out
and
in
out
and
in

lunch has stopped to
wash its trembling
whiskers
with pale pink claws
(O look behind you double
quick! Shshshsheila's nose is up
in the air nostrils flaring)

Double giggles
from the two-headed monster
awake from their naps
there's work to be done:
load the fish bowl with
trucks and blocks
drop handfuls of peanuts
on the bunny's back
and take the snakey snake
out for a walk
Shshshsheila's so grateful
to be out

O
the
hunger
hunger
hunger
of it all
snake hunger
is the worst of the worst
jungle hunger
Amazon hunger

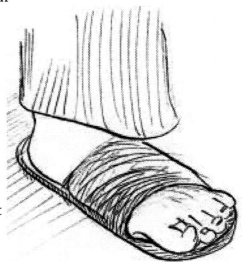

Shshshsheila mentally unhinges
her jaws
time to eat!

Duchess the Dog banished
baddog to the yard sniffs the air
and bays and bays
snake and mouse up her nose
can't someone understand my
barks she asks could someone go
after that snake for me? She runs
and runs in circles and circles
won't someone please care as
deeply as me she barks

Where is Mom?
O Where is Mom?
Guardian of the Gates
Protector of the Hearth?
where is she when a snake's loose?
Dad's asleep
brother Dan deep in the books
no one knows that a cage door
swings back and forth
back and forth
open to the breeze.

That two-headed monster
Larry&Rick
bellies full fingers licked
slides laughing laughing

Snake's Loose!

down high chairs
pick me up pick you up laughing
catch the snakey snake by the tail
time again

Only Duchess baddog knows the
truth and bays and bays
to anyone who will listen
the neighbor on the right makes
plans to call the police
the neighbor on the left makes
plans to poison the dog

Duchess, the one truly
obedient child of the house runs
back and forth back and forth
in the yard fretting where is
everyone?
Loyalty her first gift sprung
from the pound she never
will forget her gratitude
why won't this family listen?

Shshshsheila
looks
blinks
and mouse-y leaps
two steps at a time
freedom's upstairs
Toddler hands
miss pulling at

snake-y Shshshsheila's
tail she double S-curves
up this stair
and double S-curves
up that stair to the
bedrooms

Mousey mousey little mouse
has run from any more
science experiments
drops of water on his head:
can he tell it's raining?
crumbs in a bottle:
can he crawl out
with it stuffed in its mouth?
brother Dan has run his last
mouse experiment
he will not be famous
in his lifetime

busy busy frantic
paw claws
pile high the
barricade
between the southiest of South American
the pampiest of pampas snakes
and experimental
grade-A all American mousey

never going back,
never never going back

Snake's Loose!

mouse-y mouse vows
these paw claws will build a
barricade high high and higher
between mouse and snake

Up the stairs come the goggly
googly goggle-eyed
toddly toddling toddlers
spit dripping snot smiling
slimy slippery toddlers
slip sideways then down up the
stairs laughing
diapers low chins high
up the stairs they go to find
Shshshsheila
bare fat feet
stamp stamp stamp
up the stairs see them go
round tummies poke over
droopy diapers
one finger in nose
the other deep in diaper doo

Shshshsheila twists herself
up to her fullest and
tallest of heights
South America in her blood
the pampas in
her brown markings
the Amazon
surges

surges
through her spine
the tongue
the tongue
the tongue goes
out
and
in
out
and
in
watch out baby feet!
look out chubby feet!
this snake means business!

And where's Dad?
Where's Dad?
sleeping in the fattest chair
heavy sleeping head falling
up
and
down
on
chest
snores to wake the neighborhood
No one to see the
double S-curves this way
and double S-curves that way
Shshshsheila
and toddlers in the way

Snake's Loose!

Mean as a hungry dog
Shshshsheila swoops and dives
her tongue striking at
fat toddler feet
up
and
down
up
and
down
the feet stamp time
tickle tickle tickle they roar
stamp stamp stamp
bare feet on bare floor
the snake swoops and dives
South America raging
in the blood
the pampas sing in her veins!
the Amazon
surges
through her spine

stamp and giggle
stamp and giggle
tickle tickle tongue flicks
out
and
in
tickle tickle tickle
oh my baby games

Shshshsheila darts sideways
mousey mousey little mouse runs
for quick quivering cover
pulling the rug on top of her

the scent of mouse up her nose
Shshshsheila throws herself like
a spear at the quivering vermin

That two-headed monster grabs
two times for snakey snakes tail
falling down they tumble
fat feet sliding down the stairs
oh look there's
baddog to chase!
come race through the kitchen!
come see
neighbor on the left has red
blood dripping steak all zippy
with poison laced through and
through
baddog Duchess ready ready for
a nice tasty treat

Oh come here nice dog
Oh come here loud dog
loud yapping dogs get
hungry
hungry
hungry
all the work they do

all the barking a dog must do
to keep the family safe so
bad burglars don't break in
my my baddog
yes yes baddog
it's time for a

mouth snazzling

throat fizzling

tummy hissling

once and for all
thanks for the barking treat

That two headed monster
Larry&Rick grabs for the
doggy treat
snake catching and
mouse hunting and nap time
makes a toddler hungry time
when

Mom walks in two hands full of
four grocery bags
Dad's sleeping head falling on
his chest snoring loud enough to
wake the neighborhood
she says loud loud louder than
even yapping dog

what's wrong with that dog
time to take her back to the
pound don't care if it breaks
their hearts

Where are the twins she roars?
up snaps Dad's head
swallows one last snore
eyes flutter as
mousey mouse leaps to safety
outdoors as the
screen door slams shut and
Shshshsheila
slams head into wall
who let the garter snake out
bellows Mom holding
twelve inches of modest snake
in hand a question mark
in the air
who's a garter snake? thinks
Shshshsheila deeply miffed
brother Dan will kill anyone
who touches his snakes

baddog Duchess come!
baddog sniffs and tosses the
poison-laced steak away
who needs poison-laced steak
anyway?

Snake's Loose!

Come
come shouts Mom
come try some tasty
liver honey with real raspberry
kidney doggie treats
toddler hands grab grab grab
ready for the treat
Mom flings them out
Duchess springs up and snatches
them tossed in the air
one
two
and
babies get three!

Illustrations by Carl Huggins

The Lion and The Man: A Fable

by Lindamichellebaron

LION ROAMED THE African terrain, much like other lions you might have seen in photographs in *National Geographic* magazines, or those you may have witnessed during TV shows and in the movies. Although he looked similar to the captive lions you see in your local zoo, he was definitely unlike them in that he was free, born free, free as the wind blows, free as the grass…well you probably get my drift. And yes, he roared a wild, untamed, "I can chew you up for dinner as easily as I can pick my teeth" roar. He roared upon waking up, and at any time or anyplace throughout the day. Usually he roared for no other reason than that he liked the sound of his deep, ferocious, macho, king-of-the-jungle tones.

I am the king.
I am king of everything!
He roared.

He looked at his reflection in the river.

"Wow, what a roar. I almost scared myself." He fluffed his furry halo with his paws. Then he thought about the last roar.

"Hum, king of everything?" That might sound a bit ostentatious, so he revised his roar to a more humble announcement of his prowess.

Think not that I am vain. Roarrr!!!
I am simply king of the African terrain. Roaarr!!

"Now, that's better," he thought. Not too loud. It was assertive but not arrogant. And it was honest. His home, Africa, was everything. He was very clear that Africa was the entire world. There was no place in the world to consider because he'd been no place else. Of course, that affirms there *is* no place else.

Lion roared, again. He considered his roar an ounce of protection, beating a pound of cure. His mother used to roar those words to him when he was a cub.

"An ounce of protection," she growled, "is worth a pound of cure."

Lion remembered himself as a cute little cub. He remembered being the cutest little cub that you ever did see. Anyway, he envisioned his own large, beautiful, golden eyes looking up at his mother. His cubby ears would perk up as she shared her bellows of vigilance. Yet, he had to admit, he had no idea what the saying meant, "A pound of cure?" "What, pray tell, is a pound of cure?"

But, no matter, today was the day he envisioned way back then, when he, Lion, could and would roar his own frightening roar. He would growl out his own personal ounce of protection. He would roar a mean enough, loud enough, frightening enough roar that would keep the other animals "on their toes," so to speak. Wait a minute...

"Yes, I will keep the animals on their paws and their toes. But not on those weak little toes like Man has. Man doesn't even have retractable claws. Every animal knows that Man is the strangest, weakest, weirdest, creature of them all."

Lion, the king of the jungle and his mother knew the other animals, the plebeians of the jungle, must be reminded at every possible moment not to even consider the possibility of interfering in any way with the lion.

Go Lion! You're the Man!
Go Lion! Go Lion!
ROOOAAARRR!!!

"Oh, my goodness, no! Did I say 'the Man'?" Lion realized he must be hanging around Man's campsite too much. "In fact," he thought to himself, "what are plebeians, anyway?"

He must have overheard some man use that term. Lion didn't respect much of what Man had to say or do, but this word "plebeian"… that word just roars off your tongue. So, he decided to keep it in his list of favorite words.

"Pleeebeiannns" he roared again. "Pleeebeeianns!"

Lion looked again at his reflection. What a fabulous furry halo.

"It frames my face perfectly."

As he looked at his reflection he noticed some of the other jungle animals behind him. He heard their meek, weak tones. Lion wondered why they even bothered to speak. He lifted his head and turned toward them. They scattered. He roared, victoriously,

They run in fear for they know I reign.
Plus they are jealous of my fabulous mane.

Then he shook his wild, magnificent mane. Yes, it was a beautiful sight. Unfortunately, none of the animals of the kingdom had actually noticed his mane. They were furiously scrambling in order to get out of the way of his ear-deafening roar.

When Lion returned to his reflection, he noticed an unsettling sight. Man was in back of him, with one of those long powerful noisemakers they keep next to them, even when they sit relaxed at their campsite.

"What is he doing here, in my jungle?"

Now, Lion was angry. He allowed Man to stay in a section of the jungle he had set aside for them. Man was officially out of his assigned area. How dare he? Lion prepared to roar. His lean, muscular body braced. Lion glanced at the reflection of his large, imposing frame one more time before he let Man have it.

Roaarrr!!!!
I am the king of the jungle you better fear
If you know what's good for you, you'll disappear.
Roarrrr!!!!!

He was so confident that Man would run away that he returned immediately to his favorite activity, looking at his own reflection. But what he saw in the background was unbelievable.

He asked himself, "What is Man still doing here?" To add insult to injury, Man was pointing the noisemaker right at him.

"This is too much. I'll just have to give him one of my most terrifying roars."

Roarrrr!!! Roarrr!!!! Roaarrr!!!
I am King...

...Silence.

Lion couldn't move. He didn't know where he was. He wasn't bleeding. Lion couldn't tell if he had been hurt. He couldn't feel anything. But there were bars all around him. Everything smelled like Man. Lion could not believe his senses. But it was true. He was in Man's campsite. But how?

He saw Man with the noisemaker in one hand and something else in the other. Man handed the something else to the other man with him. Then Man walked over to the bars, stood right next to Lion, pointed the noisemaker towards the sky and placed his hand on Lion's mane.

Lion couldn't believe it. Man patted the top of his head the same way he played with the tame dog at the campsite. How humiliating! Lion couldn't stand still for this. Lion knew he would frighten Man's hand off his mane when he growled his ferocious roar. Lion tried to shake his mane, and growl his mighty roar, but nothing. He couldn't move. He couldn't even whimper.

The other man pointed the something or other at them and a light flashed right in Lion's face. What was amazing was what Lion saw after the flash. As the men stood together looking at the contraption, Lion could see his own reflection. Only it was a reflection of a very, very small…him and Man. It was amazing, but horrible. How could Man do that? Was there a tiny river in that thing that could magically make everything smaller and then hold it there in place?

This was unbelievable, but there it was. It was very small but he could see it clearly, in fact, too clearly. At least his eyes were working, Lion thought. It seemed to Lion that was all that was working. He, Lion, king of the jungle, was behind bars. And Man looked as if…as if…he were the ruler, standing over him, noisemaker in hand, proud and powerful.

This was the first time Lion saw his own reflection and hated what he saw. He wanted that contraption so he could make the reflection show the truth. He, Lion, was the king and Man was nothing.

During the long trip, caged, to wherever Man was taking him, Lion worked to regain his roar. He roared a "much louder than ever before" roar. He growled an "open up that caged door" roar! Finally, yes, he had it back. A more frightened than frightening little man peeked in and squeaked, "Sounds like the lion is ready to get out of here. You better come and get him!"

Roarrrrrrrrrrrrrrrrrrrr
That's right, get me out of here,
Before I give you something to really fear!

Lion showed more and more of his sharp teeth with every roar. Then he roared one last horrific roar, and the cage door swung open.

"I wish my mother could see me now. It takes three or four men to try and tie me up. But I won't give up. "Roar. Growl. Roar. Growl."

The men tied Lion up, but Lion hadn't given up. He clawed and growled until the men finally released him into a habitat that looked just like his home. Lion shook his mane defiantly, and then he surveyed his surroundings.

"This looks just like my African savannah," Lion thought as he walked around his new home. "That's what I'm roaring about!" Lion started to run, like he used to do, but no matter what direction he ran in, he ran out of space. A moat stopped him in his tracks. He was definitely not in Africa. Then Lion heard a whimper. No, that couldn't be him. There must be a cub around here someplace. He'd look later. But he had to admit he wasn't particularly pleased about the shortage of space. Africa never ran out of space to run.

"Well, it doesn't matter," he convinced himself. "I may not be home, but one thing is clear, *Man is scared of me.* Look at what lengths he's gone to make me feel at home." Lion stood stoically. Then he started to prance. He couldn't run far but he could prance. He pranced around to a chant he started making up in his head.

The Lion and The Man: A Fable

Go Lion, you're the winner.
Go Lion, you're the winner.

"Yes," he congratulated himself, "I have Man just where I want him. It's about time he knows who's the boss. Well then, I better train him correctly. It's time to let Man know that I need to be served."

Hurry up, get me something to eat.
And it better be some fresh killed meat.
Roar, roar, ROARRRR!!

Before Lion's most horrific roar raged through the habitat, he saw a man slink into the background and place something that smelled particularly tasty way off to the side.

"He's afraid," thought Lion, "as well he should be. Good. Next time I'll have him bring it closer to me." Lion walked casually, coolly, toward the scent.

"I'm training them to be great servants. Fresh meat, just as I demanded, ready for me to sink my teeth into." He sauntered over to his food and then looked up. Lion was stunned. No creature had ever watched Lion eat. The animals were all afraid if they stayed too close for too long they would be next. But here there were all kinds of Men watching him, skinny men, fat men, little men, hairy men, dark men and light men. All of them were staring at him. There were even some of the lumpier looking men that he had not seen before. They had different size lumps in several distinct areas of the body. Weird! Some of the lumpy ones and the regular looking men, held tiny replicas of themselves. "I wonder if they are like our cubs?" Lion mused.

All of them looked at Lion in awe. So, Lion reared his head up, shook his mane and growled a fierce and frightening roar.

The men jumped into one another. Lion couldn't keep himself from laughing. He felt like dancing to the beat of his new chant,

Go Lion, you're the winner.
Go Lion, you're the winner.

"They are so afraid of me that they have a moat all around this whole area to separate me from those scaredy men." Lion roared and roared and ROARED his laughter.

Some of the men held tiny boxes, like the one that had showed that embarrassing reflection of Lion and Man, back when he was in his African kingdom.

"I'll give them the real reflection of me, this time." Lion fluffed his furry halo with his paws, posed, majestically, for a moment, and then growled. The men jumped, again.

"What entertainment! But I think I'm hungry, now." Lion barely had the thought before he recognized the scent of fresh meat coming from the same area where he had previously retrieved his meal. "Right on time! All I have to do is think about it, and here it is."

After Lion devoured his meal, he looked around his new home, and smiled inside himself. That's the only way a lion should smile, on the inside. The outside of a big cat is no laughing matter. It wasn't long before Lion started to strut, a proud majestic strut. "Well, well, well," Lion thought as he swaggered through his man-made kingdom, "One thing is certain, Man knows, 'Who's the *man* around here.'"

Then Lion roared a loud, obtrusive yawn to signal his desire to rest, took one more look at his brave new world, and closed his eyes for an early evening catnap.

Percival Zeart

by M. Kaskel

THE FIRST THING that Percival ever saw was his mother's beak. It was the fourth day he had been chipping away at his shell and he could see his mother as a black and white blur through the cracks.

"OK," said Percival's father, "I'll take a turn now on the egg."

"Oh dear," said his mother, "I don't see how much longer we can keep this up! Four days now, Simone only took three. Oh dear, oh dear."

She moved to the side and let her husband move into position over the cracked egg.

"Go on," he urged her, "go get some food from the keepers, the egg is safe. I've got my wind back now."

Even though Percival's family was separated from the rest of the colony at the zoo, there were still whispers in the penguin community on how long Percival was taking. Comments on how much attention the egg was getting from Dr. Sandee, the zoo's chief veterinarian, and the keepers.

Day five came and went and Percival's dad still sat, the feathers worn off on the lower part of his belly that warmed the egg.

On day six Percival poked his head fully through the shell.

The first thing he saw with reasonable clarity was Dr. Sandee's huge smile, distorted through the magnifying glass she held.

It might have startled the average person, but Percival was

45

not a person, he was a penguin chick, and hadn't a clue there might be any danger in a human, so he was not afraid.

His proud father traded places with his mom and waddled off to feed and brag with the other penguins. His mother was well rested and overjoyed about Percival's finally being out of his shell. Dr. Sandee had just fed the penguins their krill, tiny shrimp-like food, and Percival's mom now had a belly full of the regurgitated krill and TLC to feed her new chick.

She opened her mouth wide and bent down to Percival who practically put his whole head in his mom's mouth to get at the lovely meal.

Ah! and yum! Percival's first meal was just that, indescribably delicious. He was tucked warm and cozy beneath his mother's belly at just the right height to reach into her throat.

Dr. Sandee never had a doubt there was something special about Percival. His name began with the letter P just like his father Peppy and his grandfather Penchant. The family last name was Zeart, derived from the names of the first chinstrap penguins in his family that had a chick in captivity, Zek and Articia. Zek and Articia had come from Antarctica. It was an amazing thing that Penchant had been born in the zoo, a first of its kind then.

Now, though fascinating, it was pretty much the same routine with new chicks. The parents are separated from the rest of the colony until the chick has shed his down and grown his first swimming feathers.

But, Percival had taken an extra long time to hatch and Dr. Sandee wanted to know why. Had they done something wrong with the colony at the zoo? Did they get something extra in the fish, like high mercury or some other chemical?

She tried not to get too close to Percival in the first month. So it wasn't for lack of looking that it took two weeks to see the second unusual thing about Percival.

It was sort of a birthmark placed almost directly in the middle of his little chick chest. The down was darker gray in that spot and the skin underneath was reddish in color giving the look of a purplish rough-edged heart.

After about a month, the chicks were usually ready to be hand-fed. But Percival was still so small that Dr. Sandee was reluctant to move him, even though his parents sorely needed a little break themselves.

"Perhaps we ought to try and feed him more," said Mr. Zeart, "He just seems smaller than I remember, my dear. Is that normal for a boy?"

"Oh, so what if he's a little smaller than his sister, you can't compare chicks. He is what he is."

"Maybe it has to do with that unusual thing on his chest?"

"We're all a little different," said his mother, "It's just a slight…"

"Slight?" said his father, "you call that slight? It's as big as my beak, what if it gets bigger, it'll make him a moving target in the water!"

"Oh don't be ridiculous, there aren't any whales here, nor seals. I haven't heard tell of anything else in the water here but those other kinds of penguins all our lives. Those are tales from your grandfather."

"I guess you're right, Salt. No need to worry, except that some girl will find him handsome like you found me."

Percival's mother giggled, "Peppy, it wasn't your looks that attracted me, it was the rock you brought and the way you threw it at my feet that made my heart skip a beat. I hope we're feeding him enough."

One day Percival was taken from his mother. Percival saw the big familiar face come very close. He was grasped in smooth, warm squeaky hands and immersed in a bucket. It was most distressing to be taken from his parents but not unpleasant as Dr. Sandee was gentle and kind. She gave him nice small pieces of food. It tasted different from his parents' food, bland, not as tangy.

Dr. Sandee didn't keep Percival away for long, not wanting to scare him. She always weighed and measured Percival after her son got there and had him write down the numbers in the ledger as she called them out.

Rob was good at noticing things. He noticed that Percival was slowly gaining weight and height without even looking at the ledger. He'd noticed that there was something special about him, right from the start. He noticed the differences in all the penguins and easily remembered their names and markings.

The average person could see Percival's birthmark, but Rob noticed something else, something he couldn't quite put his finger on.

Rob Sandee came to the zoo every day after school. It had started when he had gotten too old for day care and too young to leave at home alone.

Ms. Marion Peltz, the zoo director, had no problem with Rob helping out. They always needed extra help and free volunteers were fewer during the school season.

The zoo was not doing well. People came often in the summertime but once school started the numbers trickled down and though they had lots of school groups coming through, funds were tight.

Ms. Peltz was always looking for ways to bring money to the zoo. She was ecstatic when she saw Percival's birthmark. "Get that little one out with the others as soon as possible, we need the draw he'll bring."

Dr. Sandee didn't think Percival was ready. The other juveniles sometimes picked on the slightly different ones. They'd have to be careful that Percival was not pushed into the water before waterproof feathers had grown in to replace his chick down.

She let his family go out with the rest of the birds on Marion's urging.

As far as the penguins could tell Percival's first day out was not unlike the first day back with the colony for any new chick. The gossip had calmed down a bit after Percival's extended birth, but as soon as they saw Percival's birthmark the jokes and comments started.

"Your mom must've seen somethin' pretty awful to get a mark like that!" said one bird.

"Your dad must've sat too hard on you when you were an egg!" said another.

Percival didn't know how to take it all. He spent his time as close to and under his parents as possible. But they began to push him to go to the keepers on his own to get krill.

"But Mom, yours is sooooo much better."

"Thank you, dear, but we all have to get our dinner from the keepers when we're grown up, and you'll come to enjoy that just as much."

But before Percival had even reached the keepers toddling beside his mother, the lights in his eyes made him squint to see where he was going.

There seemed to be a lot of activity going on the human side of the penguin house, with lots of human voices.

"Geez, what is all this human nonsense?" said Mr. Zeart.

"It's alarming," said another penguin dad, "that marking is

bringing a lot of commotion, I knew that kind of thing would be bad news for the colony."

"That's ridiculous," Mrs. Zeart replied, "our chick is going to be a blessing to this colony as all chicks are, you wait and see."

Ms. Peltz was pleased as punch with the crowds, and the media attention. Three of the five local channels had come to the event to cover the penguin chick's story. "Penguin with a Heart" the story line read.

"Waddaya think caused this?" asked one reporter.

"Well, anomalies occur all the time in nature," said Dr. Sandee, "that's how we evolve. But what is just different here in the zoo could make an animal vulnerable in the wild. Penguins are black on one side and white on the other so that they are invisible to predators from the top and bottom in the water."

The rest of the local channels followed, sending reporters to cover the story from different angles. Some asked the visiting children what they thought about Percival. Some stations consulted experts to discuss Percival's unusual birthmark, debating its cause and implications which sparked side topics such as the value of keeping wild animals in zoos at all. They interviewed representatives from various animal welfare organizations and humane groups. Whether pro or con, they all loved the attention Percival brought to them and their causes.

Soon the national channels picked up the story, and Percival's picture went round the world on TV and online.

For the zoo, Percival Zeart was a hearty success.

The day the incident happened seemed average to the average

person without Rob's noticing abilities. Rob could sense the difference with the older chicks in the crèche. They had been skittish with their feedings and irritable with each other since Percival's presentation date. The keepers had a tendency to favor Percival when giving out the krill. It wasn't Percival's fault. The keepers just noticed that they got a lot more attention from the media when they fed Percival first.

"How come you get more food than anyone else?" Squirt poked his flipper at Percival and tried to push him aside.

"I don't mean to. Here, you go first." Percival stood aside to let Squirt and others past him.

But Janet, the keeper, just went around the group to get near Percival again. "Poor little Zeart," she pouted, "everybody is pushing in front and you are getting slighted."

"There she goes again!" huffed one of the smaller chicks. "I'll never get anything at this rate!"

"Yeah," said another, "just cause the rest of us don't have weird markings doesn't mean we should starve!"

They all began to grumble and squawk and poke at Percival. They closed in together and began to inch him toward the water's edge.

Percival's first taste of water was not the usual one for a penguin. His swimming feathers were not all filled in yet, so he soaked very quickly. He naturally started flailing around with his feet and flippers. He wanted to get back to the shoreline.

"Oh my goodness!" his mother screeched when she saw him and she made a mad dash to go in after him. Pushing through the chick pack she inadvertently knocked the chicks closest to the water's edge in. His father came running as well, along with the parents of other chicks who were now flapping about frightened, knocking even more barely covered chicks into the water.

When Rob first noticed the commotion he saw Mr. Zeart push aside a penguin chick, who in turn pushed another chick, who pushed another and another. It reminded Rob of the soldier line of the dancing Rockettes with the first one falling on the next and knocking them all down. He had already been ready with the net when he had seen the chicks jostling for position.

Janet had just kept throwing the krill, until the splashes had started.

Rob was already fishing with the net, for Percival first, and then the other chicks, as fast as he could net them.

"Mom, Mom!" Rob yelled. He knew they needed to get the chicks dried off. "Janet, get towels!"

Janet ran behind the penguin set and came back with towels. She started drying. Rob grabbed a towel and started on Percival.

Rob was mad at himself. "Geez, I knew it! I hope these chicks are OK. Mom thought it was too soon to bring Percival to the crèche."

What's the point of noticing if you can't do anything about it? He thought of his grandmother. She had been sick longer than anyone had realized. Rob could tell, but didn't know what to do about it. By the time the doctors had figured it out, it was too late.

And here it was again. His tummy told him "Watch out," and all he could do was get the net quick.

"Geez," he said to himself, looking down into Percival's eyes as he dried Percival's gray down that was beginning to molt to swimming feathers.

"Sweet little Zeart, what is it about you?"

When Percival had hit the water, he'd held his breath without even thinking. The cool water soaked his down and he was wet to the bone in two seconds flat.

Then the others came tumbling on him. Most of them just swam away. Then he felt the net from beneath and he was out in the air with a warm towel around him in no time.

He looked up at the human's eyes. He could see himself in them.

He realized what he was seeing and tried to see the mark on his chest that everyone was always talking about. "What good was it?" he thought. His mother was always so positive, but it just seemed to make him different from all the other chicks and to annoy everybody. Nobody liked him.

"Wow," said Janet, "that was fast! How'd you get the net there so quick?"

Rob just ignored her. He wasn't in the mood for explaining himself.

In a few weeks Percival's swimming feathers had finally grown in. His birthmark was lighter, but still clearly visible.

One summer morning Dr. Sandee took him in to measure him. "He's such a star," she said to her son. "This year the zoo may actually wind up in the black because of you." She patted Percival's head. "The board is discussing upgrading the penguin set, and putting in a web cam."

She handed him to Rob.

"Wow he's gotten so much heavier, I guess he'll be going for his first real swim soon."

"Yes, and, put him down, I want to look at his walk."

Rob put him down on the floor next to the shiny stainless cabinet.

"There's something about how he looks at me, Mommy, like he's looking for something in my eyes."

"Hmm. I think your affection for Percival is causing you to give him human attributes."

"Oh Mom really! Look, look how he's looking at the cabinet. Do you think he knows it's his own reflection?"

"I doubt it. Probably thinks it's another penguin if he recognizes it as a reflection at all."

Percival wobbled back and forth a bit on the cold stone floor. It was very flat under his feet as opposed to the bumpy pseudo arctic floor of the penguin pen.

He caught the movement of a penguin shape out of the corner of his eye and wondered who else might be in here with Dr. Sandee. But then he had a closer look, really close. He saw this penguin had what he had never seen on any other one in the crèche: a mark on its chest. A mark shaped like two shrimp stuck together at the head and filled in.

He knew pretty quickly that he was looking at his own reflection.

"Oh, it's HUGE," thought Percival. "What female chick is going to find me interesting with this huge blob on my chest?" He started to sulk. His mom had always given him so much hope, but there it was in black and white, the thing his father talked about and probably thought Percival had never heard his concerns.

Rob picked up Percival and looked close at his face again. "Is there intelligent life in there or what?" he said. His mother laughed. She always laughed at his attempts to be funny.

Rob took Percival back to the pen. There was a young artist named Brad repainting the background of the arctic landscape. The zoo had been just able to squeeze the cost of the painting into their budget. Things had definitely improved with the crowds that Percival drew, but as his heart faded with each molting, Ms. Peltz worried about losing the crowds again. Dr. Sandee worried about the research she was doing and Rob worried because he couldn't figure out what it was that was different about Percival beyond his birthmark.

The artist was working on painting the sun, with orange, yellow and white beams shooting through the clouds. Rob thought he ought to be working with a barrier because the penguins might knock over the art supplies, but he didn't want to be a nag, especially considering his age. So he brought some paper towels and a bucket from the back room and placed it near where the artist worked.

Janet came out to feed the birds, but she had developed a crush on the artist and was trying to flirt with him while she worked.

"Brad, it's looking so brilliant. Just like the National Geographic photos of the terrain. Have you looked at it on the web cam?"

Brad flirted back. "Oh thanks, thanks, yeah I did a lot of research."

The eyelash batting and giggles went back and forth. Janet was looking at Brad and not at the krill she was throwing. The little ones were all at her feet and all of a sudden she was falling back over the plaster rocks. Brad dropped the orange paint and brush to catch her and suddenly there were little black and white penguins everywhere as the krill flew.

Orange feet in orange paint, a disaster! Luckily Rob had brought the paper towel and bucket out. After helping Janet up, Brad filled the bucket of water from the pool. They all started grabbing penguins as they scrambled around for the spilled krill. Rob was there to catch the penguins as they walked through the paint, scoop them up, dunk them in the bucket, wipe their feet and mop up the paint. It would take some time to clean up the mess, they would probably have to drain the tank and refill it now.

Percival had been watching Brad and his brush for days. Today he was painting a shape with the same color orange as his feet. Percival liked something about the shape. He didn't know what. He just liked it.

When Janet came out to feed everyone, as usual, Percival kept to the back so there wouldn't be a ruckus. But a ruckus happened anyway. Janet fell and there was krill and the foot-colored goo everywhere. Percival walked in the orange stuff to go after a bit of krill that had flown his way. He noticed it stuck to his feet and then to the ground leaving the foot color. He carefully began to move his feet one step and then another next to it, making the shape he liked. He was busy, totally absorbed in his steps when he was picked up and dunked in the bucket; and all the lovely color was gone.

Two seconds after Rob grabbed Percival to get the paint off his feet he saw it, the arc of orange footprints. He was sure Percival had made it and it looked like he wasn't finished. In fact, it looked remarkably like the sun that Brad had been working on before the disaster. And then it was gone! Brad had knocked over the bucket and started mopping up the orange paint before it dried on the rocks.

"Did you see that?" he yelled at Brad. "He was copying your sun!"

"Oh, don't be ridiculous, Rob, he's a penguin. I know he's special, but really."

"Ohhhh," Rob said out loud. Then he grumbled to himself, "They never believe me, but they're glad I'm there with the bucket." He put Percival down and pushed him until he was at the edge of the pool. "Come on buddy, it's time you had a swim." Rob knew Percival's swimming feathers weren't fully grown in but he'd never seen a penguin with such reluctance to swim.

There he was, being pushed to the water's edge. "Go on." His mother called to him.

Percival leaned forward, put his flippers in the air and took a jump.

"Yeah!" his parents yelled for joy, flapping at their sides.

It was glorious, the feel of water streaming against his swimming feathers. He naturally pushed with his flippers and feet and it was easier and more pleasurable than he had believed it could be. Only Percival really knew how much fear he had overcome to take that plunge. The incident months before, when he still had his chick down, had scared him. With that, in addition to the tales about whales and sharks, he was still apprehensive. But he had faith that it was safe here at the zoo. It seemed so silly now that he had been afraid at all.

Rob told his mother about the sun that he thought Percival was painting. She sounded doubtful, but she was a scientist. "Do an experiment, test your theory about Percival's art," she told her son, "but you'll have to find a way that's safe for the penguin."

Rob found some paint labeled non-toxic. He took a picture of the sun on the penguin set and taped it to the inside of an enclosed pen on the floor of the backroom. He spread papers on the floor of the pen. While his mother watched, he got Percival and dipped his feet in a plate of the paint, and set him down in the pen.

Percival was startled to have his feet dipped in the cool paint.

He didn't know what the humans were doing. He looked around the enclosed area Rob had just put him in. There on the side of the wire fence was hanging the familiar shape that was on the wall of the penguin set. Percival just stood for a while. There wasn't anywhere to go. He stared down at his feet and saw the foot colored, foot shapes that he had seen the other day. He realized that he was making them with whatever Rob had put on his own feet and he remembered the pleasure of copying the sun shape, so he did it again one little step next to the other while turning.

And there it was pretty close to the shape in the picture.

Suddenly Rob gave him a piece of shrimp. What joy he felt. Why, he didn't know.

Rob and his mom were flabbergasted. "He's an artist!" he said.

"I can't believe it!" she said. "Now wash his feet off... I know it's non-toxic but paint on feet is too unnatural for me."

Rob picked up Percival, then dipped him and washed off his feet in the utility sink.

He took Percival back to the penguin set. "Percival made art!" he told Janet.

"What do you mean?"

"I put paint on his feet like it was the other day and he copied Brad's sun on paper."

"Wow," said Janet, "let me see it."

"It's in the backroom."

They went around where Dr. Sandee was staring at Percival's art. "Just amazing," she repeated. She picked up the phone on her desk and punched a number.

"Marion, I have something amazing to tell you. Well, I rather let you see for yourself... come down to the backroom."

Ten minutes later Ms. Peltz appeared, slightly breathless. "What,

what is it?"

"Look." Dr. Sandee showed her Percival's art. "The penguin, Percival, did it himself…we just dipped his feet in the paint and he did the art."

"You dipped his feet in paint?"

"Nothing harmful. My son noticed something when the paint disaster happened the other day. What's more, he actually copied the artist's sun from the penguin set…see?" she showed Ms. Peltz the print-out of the photo.

"Amazing," said Ms. Peltz.

"Amazing," said Dr. Sandee.

"Amazing," said Janet and Rob together.

"I'll send out a press release," said Ms. Peltz.

"Oh no!" Dr. Sandee worried.

"Don't worry," said Ms. Peltz, "we won't overdo it, don't want to overtax our little Zeart heart!"

Dr. Sandee smiled.

"We can do T-shirts and note cards; I'll have to find a designer…" Ms. Peltz' voice trailed off as she walked down the hall.

Suddenly she rushed back in, "Oh, I almost forgot. I got a call from an international penguin group. They have a couple of young birds they'd like us to take in. Refugees from that oil spill last week."

"Fantastic," Dr. Sandee said, "what kind of shape are they in?"

"Oh, an oily mess; strained and broken flippers, the usual injuries from oil slicks.

"I'll get back to you on that after I write that press release." Ms. Peltz rushed off again.

The day of the press conference was exciting for Rob. All the local TV stations and two cable stations had reporters and cameras. The papers had reporters with notepads and photographers. There was a special group of grammar school reporters and students.

"Ladies and gentlemen, thanks to Rob Sandee's gift for observation, we now know about Percival's gift for art."

Rob beamed, his mother beamed. Percival just blinked and hadn't a clue.

Rob dipped his feet in paint just as he had before and Percival made the shape just as before. All the cameramen and reporters oohed and aahed and said, "amazing." Rob gave Percival a nice piece of shrimp, washed his feet and put him back in the penguin set where he promptly went for a swim.

Then it was time to present the new penguins.

Professor Kendall came to the podium set up in front of the penguin set especially for the occasion. "Thanks to your interest and the refurbished penguin house, I saw Percival and the special colony here first on the Internet. A few weeks ago these two penguins were rescued from the oily waters near to the spot the tanker ran aground. Ms. Peltz and Dr. Sandee have generously consented to allow them to make their new home here at the Central Zoo. Ladies and gentlemen, may I present Morty and June."

Two penguins waddled out into the penguin set. They both had sweaters on. "The sweaters are to keep them from preening the oil and swallowing it. They'll keep them warm and act like natural skin oils until their new feathers grow in. The salt water will gradually deteriorate the sweaters."

The reporters asked lots of questions about the oil spill and how the penguins were rescued. Professor Kendall explained their injuries, June had a broken leg and the veterinarians with the rescue group had devised a special waterproof splint for her. She limped when she waddled. Morty had a sprained flipper and his vision was damaged but the professor explained he ate krill just as readily as any other penguin.

"Are they a couple?" one of the school reporters asked.

"No, they are not mates at present, we believe they are just a little too young, so hopefully neither has been separated from a mate. Much of their colony was damaged by the oil slick and it is sad but likely that these little ones will never go back to the wild."

Many more questions were asked and answered. Then the line of visitors started. Dr. Sandee was beaming, enjoying her son's success.

The moment Percival had seen June he got a feeling almost as good as making the shape with his feet; mixed with sort of a nervous flutter, the way he had felt before he took his first plunge into the pool. He waddled over to meet her along with the other members of the community. Many of them kept some distance. Her feathers had an odd look about them and she had a thick leg and funny walk. But since the day that Percival had first discovered the joy of making foot shapes he didn't care what anyone else thought. He was still self-conscious about his mark, but it had faded slightly with each molting and he had long since gotten used to the remarks.

He took a gulp and approached. "Welcome, I'm Percival. Where have you come from?"

"I'm June," she answered. "Morty and I have been away from our colony a long time, I can't say where it is in relation to here. It was terrible, a terrible disaster." June hung her head.

Percival could tell she was sad. He wanted to comfort her. "Well, anytime you want to talk about it is OK with me. Would you like to swim?" he bravely asked.

"Aren't you worried about the whales and sharks?" she questioned. Percival knew by now she was referring to the mark on his chest.

"Nahhhh, I'm a really fast swimmer."

June looked surprised.

"Actually, I'm just kidding, there are no whales here. Just tales from the wild, my mother says. Have you actually seen a whale?"

"Oh, yes at a distance. I've seen young ones fall in, or get pushed in and they never come back, especially if they're small or...different." June wanted to be careful with her words. The mark on Percival's chest was different, but it was cute too. And he had made it to almost mating age, so perhaps it was true there were no predators here.

"I was pushed in once, when I was molting."

"My goodness, how did you get out?"

"The humans scoop us out. I wasn't in the water but a moment. It's very safe here."

June liked the sound of that, safe. After all she had seen, it seemed a long time ago and yet not. She missed her colony, but she liked the sound of safety.

Percival could see the tears well in her eyes.

They talked a lot over the next few days and she told him all about the oil spill, the cleaning, the relocation center. They spent a lot of time swimming with Morty. He and June were each other's connection to their oil-ruined colony and they had become like brother and sister to each other.

Percival felt he belonged with penguins his own age for the first time in his life. Whatever the reason the Creator had in giving him his mark didn't matter anymore. It was but a light gray now. The humans had him painting more often, and he enjoyed it. He liked that June thought he was so brave to swim with such a mark. June liked that Percival liked her, even with the oddly colored sweater the humans had made her, it was slowly unraveling every time she swam, much as Percival's mark had faded with each molting.

Then one day the knitting came off altogether. And June's lovely pattern could be seen, as it never had been before. She still wore the leg brace and maybe she always would. Percival never even noticed it.

Rob set up Percival to paint about one time a week. Dr. Sandee thought any more than that was too much. Ms. Peltz also thought it was good business to keep the number of original Zeart paintings low and the value high. There were now T-shirts and note cards, calendars and daybooks with penguin poetry decorated with Percival's art; pillow covers and needlepoint; book marks and "Percival Paints" DVDs. All of these things brought people and their pocketbooks to the zoo. All that kept the chinstraps in krill and the meerkats in crickets.

Percival no longer painted in a pen. And he didn't need the picture of the sun to copy. Rob just dipped his feet and put him down on the paper. Percival walked around step by step as usual and Rob picked him up, put the painting aside while he washed Percival's feet.

One day he moved the painting aside and then put Percival down before turning around to get a towel. And the next amazing thing happened.

Percival had picked up the paper with his beak from the rock where Rob had placed it. And he wobbled over to June and placed it at her feet. Rob caught his breath. No one else was around to witness this moment. Only he would ever see how Percival asked June to be his mate.

Percival had lifted the picture gingerly. He had never tried before. He only knew that she had said how much she liked that he enjoyed painting; that it gave her pleasure to see him so happy. The thought had struck him the moment Rob had placed his art in such an easy place to pick it up. He carried it twelve feet to June and put it down. She flapped her flippers against her side and cried for joy.

"Oh Percival, you have made me soooo happy."

Percival still had a streak of the traditional in him and so he went and picked up the rock he had put aside especially for this occasion, and dropped it in the center of the sunburst he had laid at June's feet.

They danced and called to each other and flapped their flippers for a long time.

In a few more moltings Percival's heart had faded completely to white. Any outward sign that he was different from any other penguin was gone. Percival now looked as he had wanted to when he was growing up, but it didn't matter anymore. There were two eggs to tend to. Each would take seven days to hatch.

Okay Johnson

by Chey Backuswalcott

OKAY WAS NOT happy living in a colored world. "Eeeh," he scoffed at the robin's red breast. How gauche he thought the toucan's multi-colored crest and the flowers that bloomed in the spring were. All the strutting and fluttering of the colored zoo animals bored the okapi. Even though the zoo was a landscaped, natural environment, with clusters of grasslands, savannahs, rolling hills filled with vegetation, and bodies of water; some animals, like the okapi, who were born to run freely, felt trapped. Zoo animals were divided up, usually by kind or number and surrounded by fine wire fences that dissolved into the greenery. These large expanses of land were irregularly parceled up and surrounded a core of interior walkways and gates used by keepers to feed animals and house them away from the public for the night.

Okay was clustered with a number of animals, including his dreaded enemy, the leopard. Another vexing problem for him were the larger birds, such as peacocks, which wandered freely in and out. Then there were the people that filled the outer walkways.

The okapi's tolerance for everything: the zoo, the bright colors, the noise, the lights and the parade of city life, was gone. He paced back and forth in his cramped quarters. No one really knows what a captive animal feels, unable to get out of the sun, go for a long walk, visit friends, explore the world or just hang out in the cool underbrush. "I've been here too long, simply too long," he muttered to himself. Gone were the expansive limits of his world...in the soft, muted haze...in the Wamba. In the Congo.

Okay was not born in the zoo like most of his okapi kind or like the other animals. He could remember as far back to shortly after he was born, when he stood up and wobbly walked for the first time. In a few hours he was running, leaping and sprinting through the shadowy understory of the rainforest. He loved his home under the high, high mahogany and the filtered light, the streams of light that lit his way in the tight thickets of bamboo. The beams of light that made him disappear. He loved standing between the streams, the light streams that hid him right in the open. Okay laughed and laughed inside, as he stood right in front of his enemies in the Ituri Forest. They could not see him. They'd circle around, muttering, growling. "There he is, no...yes...there...no...I saw him, I tell you. There, by the Epulu waters."

He would spin around shaking his striped hind legs, which made his lower body invisible on the forest floor. There, his uneven striping skillfully played with the shadow and light to absorb him—as if he'd vanished. His dark, velvet fur was the color of the deepest umber, almost black, like his favorite hiding place in front of the giant shaded mangrove tree. Okay's enemies could not corner him because of his odd beauty, his difference, his textures and contrasts.

But here at the zoo, Okay was the source of many cruel jokes. He had no shadows, tall tropical trees or playful light to show off his beauty, his prowess or his magical disappearances. They just didn't get it. And the concept of camouflage is hard to explain to animals who had never been wild, who had spent all their lives fenced in, who did not have to hunt or hide, nor sprint for miles to try and find the limits of their world.

All the four-legged animals were teasing him except for the giraffes. Their height made them aloof. They would bob up and down to listen in and then whisper among themselves. They kept a big secret from the other animals. They never participated in the attacks on Okay—but they did not protect him either.

"Why are you dressed up like that?" said the Bengali, Ben Tiger. "Where do you think you're going?"

"Who do you think you are? Are you trying to pass for human?" mocked Chessamachi Cheetah.

"You wouldn't say such mean and heartless things to me if we were in the wild. Would they, Wild Dog? You'd respect me, if we weren't in a zoo," Okay said, shaking his long neck from side to side. Okay raked his head back and forth against the wire gate as he sidestepped toward his hecklers. He stuck out his over foot-long tongue and wrapped it around Bubba's throat. Bubba's eyes bugged out as he gasped for air.

"Not that tough now, not so cute or fast at all, you fearless baa baby," laughed Okay. "Go beat your chest somewhere else, you bulky baboon."

"You'll never look as good as any of us," said Ben Tiger. "Look at me. My coat has beautiful, even stripes from my head to my toes—a natural pattern. My markings are dead center. I have symmetry, something you completely lack. You have no design, my good man!"

"You look pieced together, like the humans' monster Frankenstein," added Wild Dog. "Remember him from those movies? The ones they showed outdoors last summer? And Fred Astaire too. The humans watched them every night."

Now every animal was kicking and doubled over with

belly-whopping laughter. "Every one knows that animals don't wear clothes," cackled the jackal and hyena. All laughed and laughed and rolled in the grass, banging the sides of Okay's enclosure, some with their mighty hooves, others with their heavy paws.

"But, but–he he he–but, but, why are you wearing those ridiculous white socks?" wheezed Hyacinth Hyena between he he he ha ha ho.

"Yeah, yeah," whopped Chessamachi.

"The socks are the funniest part," wheezed Jasper Jackal, as tears of laughter ran down his face. "They look like the humans' knee socks complete with garters, ha ha ha ha heee… like in that Fred Astaire movie."

"Yeah, that's it," said Wild Dog, "you look like him, all you need is a top hat…ha ha."

"We'll call you Fred Astaire Frankenstein from now on," stammered Jasper.

"Don't call me that," said Okay. "I was called Okapia Woeoudi—with respect—by the hunters in my homeland. Even the white foreigners kept saying 'Okay, Okay, Okay,' as they roped me. The ropes dug into my neck, leaving burns, and cutting off my air."

"You mean your native hunters turned you in?" cackled Jasper.

"Who could forget such a terrible thing?" said Okay sadly in his whistling voice. "They used the Wambutti to hunt me. Only they knew of my existence."

"You can never trust a hunter," said Wild Dog. "They'll turn on you. They dream of seeing your blood—they smell it."

"We o'api knew they found the zebra—with its black and white striped skin," said Okay, "they were hunted mercilessly for their coats. And we knew they searched for us," Okay added in

70

hushed phrases. "Perhaps they had heard stories of o'api. We laughed while they looked for animals that looked like horses, ponies, donkeys and especially, zebra. They searched but had never seen any of us. We laughed in the forest, in the hidden places, in the Wamba. Behind the Epulu water falls.

"Then we heard the Wambutti whispering where we lay hidden deep in the forest. Some guy, Sir Harry H. Johnston, an opportunist, sent home two headbands made from the skin of a fallen o'api as if he himself had trapped the o'api. As if himself had found us."

"Hunters lie," Ben Tiger said.

"But it took him many years to get the Wambutti to give us up," Okay said. "Soon after, our necks were wrenched from lassos and our bodies were racked with the pain of spears. The outsiders gave Johnston the credit and they gave my kind the Latin name, *Okapia johnstoni*.

"I took that outsider's last name, Johnston, the name of the man who didn't find us, but who pretended he did, to help tell the story of my capture," said Okay. "Okay Johnson, Okay Johnson, you see, tells the whole story, Okay, *Okapia johnstoni*—Okay Johnson, ok?"

"Okay, Okay, Okay," chimed the others, "we get it."

Okay had awakened dry and parched and praying, as he did most mornings, for rain. Disgusted and tired with all the banter, Okay walked to the front gate and nibbled on the leaves. The people were coming by. He longed for some *dolea* and *faso* or other tangy fruit from his home in the wild that would make him mellow.

There was very little vegetation to hide in and not enough space to sprint with long leaps to get away. Instead, Okay whistled a mournful lament for his homeland and his mother. He hadn't seen her since he was born. Okay regretted that day now when he found his footing and confidently jutted away from her, eager to find his place in the world. He never even looked back or wished her farewell. It was his nature to hold no sentiment. His was a natural exile, self-imposed. But now he was sorry he'd never see her again.

But just then, two curious creatures approached his corral. One had feet and a partial striped head like a zebra and the other had spots—just like his dreaded enemy, the leopard. Instinctively, Okay shifted himself from side to side into the back, hiding in the scruffy bushes in his corral.

"Oh look," said the one with zebra stripes—Zorida—and pointed. Okay was thoroughly surprised when he realized that she could still see him. He shifted again, turning and looking over his shoulder. Now I'm certain the sweet-voiced one can't see me, he thought.

"Look, look! His stripes match mine," said Zorida. Okay darted further away, as he wondered what kind of enemy wore stripes like his to attack him. A striped enemy with a sweet human voice, what was this?

Okay had seen humans before at home in the wild when he was running free. These kind of resembled the hunters from the wild who were little and small, but those hunters hadn't been tall and big like these two. In the wild Ituri, he had run from the Mubutu and Efe for exercise. The Pygmy hunters had chased him, but they were too small to keep up with him. Okay always outran their arrows. It was a fun game for him. The Efe and Mubutu had no stripes, but they were a rich cocoa brown like he was. Could these two be large Efe or Mubutu? But they had stripes and spots.

"Can you see me now?" he blurted out, accidentally. Das yelled, "Yes, I see you, brother. I see you!" He was pointing straight at him. Oh no, Okay raced away to catch the rays of the sun. The rays would hide him, he thought.

"Can you see me now?" Okay asked. He called me brother and has stripes like me, Okay thought...and wondered, are we related?

"Yes, we can both see and hear you." Zorida told him.

"What a fun game," said Das, the one with the spots. "He's trying to play a game with us."

"I hope he doesn't think that I'm wearing his fur," said Zorida, the striped one, as she sensed Okay's fear. "Listen, my shoes and headband are not from an endangered species like you," said Zorida.

"What kind of zebra looks like that anyway?" said Das.

"Oh no, not again," whined Okay. "How many times do I have to go through this in the same day? Did Hyacinth Hyena send you to bother me? Laugh at my socks? Again?"

"No," said Zorida. "We came here from the parade to get a break from the beating sun. It's a long walk uptown."

"It's such a hot day and we're tired. We thought we'd get an icy," Das said. "—And some shade," he added.

"I know what you mean," Okay told him. "I was waiting for rain. There's no streams or waterfalls around here to run through." The okapi shook his long neck in puzzlement. "What are you?" asked Okay.

"What do you mean, what are you?" snapped Zorida. "What do we look like? It's Malcolm's birthday. We're from the parade—put two and two together, duh!"

Unfortunately, Okay understood no part of that conversation, but he did worry. The sweet one's voice had changed.

"How did you get out there?" asked Okay. "What kind of animals are you? Are you zebra? Leopard? Or are you human? I am faster and stronger than you! You can't hurt me," Okay told them.

The strangers both began to laugh like hyenas. "You're so sensitive," said Zorida "and so literal. We're in fashion. You know, fashionable. You think we look like animals," and they both laughed and laughed.

"No, no, my brother," said the one with the spots, "We are humans, who, probably from your point of view, look like animals. Ha, ha, ha!"

"Ha, ha, ha, I'm female, m' man, ha ha, so you should say— my sistah," Zorida laughed.

"Oh. Can you get me out of here, my sistah? Can I parade with you?" pleaded Okay.

"You want us to help you escape?" asked Zorida.

"But you're not domesticated," said Das, "you're wild— from the jungle."

"In New York," explained Zorida in hushed, confidential tones, "there are laws, ordinances, health codes, fear, police, rules, police, protesters, activists, police—and a thousand reasons why animals can't be free," they chimed together.

"I've never really come across anyone who is truly free," said Zorida. "Sure, the zoos create the illusion of running free, but you've seen how confined your habitat really is."

"In fact, none of us are really free—not even humans," Das added.

The two pulled back a little and began to discuss the situation in low tones. "Well, anyone who talks as well as this guy can't be but so wild," said Zorida.

"I don't know," said Das. "Suppose he attacks someone, goes crazy, eats somebody or goes berserk, like in the movies— remember King Kong? Then what are we gonna do? Plus, have you really taken a good look at him? Do you think he'll really blend in? Look at his horse-like face and body for that matter," said Das.

Zorida stopped for a minute to take a good look. "Well, you know, Das, if you look at him from this angle, he looks a little like your great uncle, Morti Myerson, when he was still alive. I know a lot of long-faced, narrowly drawn people who look like horses. Just look at that guy over there! He's a horse if I ever saw one," said Zorida, contemplating the possibilities, as they both tried to muffle laughs.

"Let's do it," said Zorida. Das nodded his agreement.

The two came nearer again. "Listen, man," said Zorida to Okay, "you gotta be cool. You can't act out, eat or kill anybody or mess up or else, we'll go to jail and you—they'll shoot you on sight. When we get to the Big H, Harlem, U.S.A., you'll blend in there."

"Don't worry man," said Das. "New Yorkers are born cool. You can walk down the street carrying a dead body, among hundreds of people, but nobody will say a thing. They're too cool, man. Nobody wants to be involved," said Das.

Okay was excited about leaving with them. He was desperate to find a place to fit in. "You won't be disappointed, my friends," said Okay, "blending in is what I do best. You'll see. Except for getting caught by the English foreigners who trapped me, I specialized in eluding my enemies at home. Even the deadly panther looked like a fool, as he wandered around looking for me, leaping and pouncing from bush to bush. I had to fight myself to keep from laughing. I was right in front of him, but I melted in with the shadowy forest." Okay pounced around the corral getting ready for anything he had to do to escape.

The giraffes motioned to him to forget the notion. They surrounded him and told him their secret in haste.

Geraldo led the confession: "Okay," he said, "we are family."

"Yes," said Ginger Giraffe. "We are cousins. As much as you are an okapi, you're really a giraffe. You're part of our family. We should have done something about the teasing and meanness of the others in the beginning. But we never thought you would leave. We're sorry we did nothing to protect you."

Then Ginger tried to stop him by telling her tale of woe—about how she tried to escape back in the day when she was a filly. Each giraffe strutted gracefully and lowered its long neck to tell him not to go. All promised to be more of a family to him if he stayed. But Okay told them no, this was his chance for freedom. Reluctantly, graceful necks swaying, they agreed to help.

A quartet of giraffes moved gracefully with the determined okapi as they looked out for the zookeepers. Because of their long necks, the giraffes always acted as lookouts for all the animals. They waited and watched anxiously, silently stretching their necks high for any sign of the keepers. But the tension eventually caused them to pace from gate to gate as they tried to anticipate where the gatekeepers would come from. The giraffes' plan was to surround Okay so he could not be seen and escort him to freedom. All would walk to the gate nearest the walkway where Okay's human friends were waiting, ready to flee. They planned to run behind the okapi from side to side in the walkway causing their outfits of stripes and spots to camouflage Okay from any pursuers. The remaining giraffes split up and waited in each corner of the corral. This would force the zookeepers to open all the gates to collect them for the night.

The rear gates opened first one by one. All the animals felt mounting tension and strain, waiting for just the right moment, when just the right gate would swing open, just wide enough, to allow for the escape.

Crowds of people were moving about. There was a woman with a screaming baby in a stroller and other women trying to find their toddling children and youngsters. Human noises escalated against the background sounds from the parade, increasing the tension of the escapees and their sense of panic. They tried to stay cool, but the right moment finally had come.

Okay bolted for freedom before anyone was ready or realized what had happened. He left in a cloud of dust, which he kicked up in his haste, as he bolted from his dusty corral.

Okay was startled by the thunderous sound he made as he moved in and out of the humans on the walkway. Clickeytee clump, clickeytee clump, click, click… Frightened by his own sound, terrorized by the thought of running into a human, Okay ran faster. The humans scared him, making him fearful, making him run faster, making him dart in and out of the crowds, on and off the walkway in his panic. It had not rained for several days and when he ran off in the dirt Okay choked on the dry earth he kicked up. He wanted to be free more than anything. His desperation made him run wildly on, not even looking back for his friends Das and Zorida, whom he had conspired with. Feeling free, Okay felt his wildness returning for the first time since he was lassoed by the neck and surrounded by white foreigners. Zookeepers took up the chase but failed to keep up.

Das and Zorida did as they promised and zigzagged back and forth as they ran, creating a blur of animal patterns as they distanced themselves in the crowd.

As they reached the street, the three quietly slipped into the parade and marched off. Not one person noticed Okay. Not one was fearful. Nor was anyone in any way concerned about Okay's appearance. He simply mixed in a crowd of multiple patterns, stripes, hues of brown, cinnamon, creams, caramels, polka dots, prints of leopard, tiger, and zebra.

Uptown was alive with sights and sounds of a festive marketplace. People were gathering all along 125th Street, Harlem's main shopping area, where sidewalk merchants were selling hats, music, art and books. Others walked in and out of boutiques and department stores. Busloads of tourists from all over the world were docking and visitors who spoke different languages dispersed among the crowd. Huge banners with gigantic people on them hung across the buildings. It was Harlem Week, the whole month long.

"Tonight is the big dance, Okay," said Zorida, high stepping to the rap music in the air. "We are going to the tailor to pick up our outfits."

"Yeah, tonight is the Black and White Ball, everyone is going," Das said.

"Here's our tailor's place," Zorida said with great excitement.

"Welcome, folks," Gianini, the shopkeeper, greeted them. "Hey, big fella. Looks like you're almost ready for tonight's ball. "Let's see," he said, sizing Okay up. "I can work with those stripes, even though they are uneven. What happened to the front? Were you in a hurry? Don't worry, big stuff, there's still time." Gianini reached for his sharpest cutters, grabbed bolts of fabric and in a whirling flurry, started to work his magic. "I studied in the great fashion houses of Paris, Milan and Spanishtown, Jamaica. No neck is too long, no butt too wide or high. I've seen it all," Gianini cackled, as he measured Okay's long neck.

Okay marveled at the place. He had never seen such interesting markings and designs before. "I like this one," he blurted out, " I knew an animal that looked like this cloth."

"Yeah, OK, boss," Gianini scoffed, "everyone's a designer these days. I will make it all hang together, my man," he muttered as he cut and spun the fabrics wildly in the air making a blur of blacks and whites, dots and stripes.

When he finished, he cheered accolades at himself. "Ya mon, I am the greatest cutter of all time: The great Gianini!"

All admired Okay's suit with oohs and ahs. Okay twirled

before the mirror. At last he had disappeared. Finally he could not see himself. Just like back home in the wild, Okay was absorbed into the background of fabric prints, stripes and orderly patterns, shelves and fashion accessories. "I almost feel at home," he said. Meanwhile, Zorida and Das slipped into their new outfits and they posed happily beside him.

"Look in the mirror at my art of skillful blending," Gianini declared. "No one could ever tell where one of you begins and the other ends. No one."

All the floats were lining up to dock on the west side of 125th Street. As they passed by, crowds of kids, residents, shoppers and tourists turned to watch. "Get your tickets here for the ball tonight," said a man dressed in black and white stripes. There were others too, selling tickets. "All aboard the *Intrepid!* Don't forget your ticket," said another. As Okay and the others left Gianini's shop, many people excited by the parade surrounded the ticket hawkers and got tickets.

"You can come with us," said Das to Okay.

"Ya man…" said Okay, bopping side to side in excitement. "I'm going to the dance and I'm going to dance the Fanga Alafia like we use to do at home in the Congo."

"Teach me that at the dance," said Zorida with Das echoing in.

"I'll be doing some advanced hip-hop myself," said Das as he began to high step to the street music. The hawker who was selling his tickets briskly, looked at Okay's outfit and said, "M' man, you are the best dressed I've seen all day. This ticket is on me."

That night, all the partygoers felt the magic as they approached the *Intrepid* pier down on the 42nd Street docks.

Aircraft on the ground and on deck were spotlighted while

searchlights panned the sky. Helicopters landed on their marked spots in the landing area and guests disembarked as the wind whipped around their flowing gowns and ballroom dresses. Men held on to their hats, ties and scarves. Flags from all nations fluttered from the ship's masts.

The trio arrived amidst all the excitement. Gianini had made Okay's outfit with a high collar of stripes and dots, which broke up Okay's long neck and made him appear shorter. Many of the characters from the floats paraded around as the guests arrived, so Okay, in his unique Gianini original, was oohed and aahed at for his highly stylized design.

The pier was the site of a huge cocktail party. Because of their festive outfits, the friends looked like the entertainers who performed throughout the crowd to keep the party lively and the guests excited. Longshoremen and members of the coast guard lined the ship's entrance and boundaries of the affair. Okay and friends mingled among the partygoers. Das and Zorida talked with friends and all took pictures with the seamen in uniform, many of whom they knew from their neighborhood.

While mingling on the pier, they ran into Das and Zorida's friends, Conrad and Larry, who had on their sparkling dress whites. Das made the introductions. Okay was interested in the uniformed men and asked, "What is it like to wear uniforms, my brothers?"

"Well, I don't mind. It bonds us together," Conrad answered.

"And I know immediately who I'm sailing with tonight by the uniform. I'll know who boards which vessel with one glance," echoed Larry.

"It's off to Africa later tonight," added Conrad. Africa! Okay felt an overwhelming excitement. He was enjoying his visit to Harlem, but Africa was home.

Here at the ball, everyone wore black and white. There were polka dots, narrow-striped and wide-striped suits of clothes.

Multi-patterned patterns, animal prints, flowers and the reverse of everything. Some wore black on the top and white on the bottom. Women fluttered by in chiffon, lamé, shiny silk charmeuse and every kind of texture imaginable. Some had huge jungle flowers sewn on solid and patterned gowns.

The music was jazzy and rhythmic and the dancing was frenetic. Zorida, Das and Okay gyrated. Everyone thought they were dancers. Groups of people with similar outfits performed coordinated dance routines. Others pranced and gyrated in and out of the dancers like acrobats in a circus. There were the glitterati in silver sequins and almost all had fairy dust sprinkled on their shoulders, arms and face. Both men and women wore pixy tinsel on their heads, which twirled all around reflecting the light. It was a spectacular sight. Huge balls of fractured mirrors whirled and the light shot off it in all directions. It was electric and Okay had never been so happy and carefree. He danced the Alafia and other moves he had learned from the Efe. He strutted his stuff as he had seen the Mubutu warriors do in their villages.

Soon, the music stopped and a long runway appeared. Out stepped Das and Zorida's tailor, Gianini, who introduced women and men wearing fabulous outfits. The crowd went wild with applause and cheers. Then Gianini began to go on and on about his most spectacular outfit of all time. The spotlight panned the crowd and finally stopped on Okay and his friends.

Okay had spent all of his life hiding. He was not ready for all the attention and became very frightened. He saw everyone stop and turn and look at him. No one ever got a good look at him, ever!

Instinctively, Okay got down on all fours and bolted through the crowd. As he ran, he could hear in his mind the jeers from Ben Tiger, Hyacinth Hyena, Chessamachi Cheetah and Bubba Baboon, "Who do you think you are?" "Why do you wear clothes?" "Do you think you're human?" "You're not human, you're not human!"

He ran and ran. The light bounced off the whirling balls, reminding him of home in the wild, where he could hide in peace on the forest floor behind the waterfalls of the Wamba.

There were so many people that Okay did not know where to turn. He darted in and out of the crowd. Finally, at the edge of the crowd, he ran into Larry the longshoreman who offered to help the frightened okapi.

"Follow me. I know what you need to do," said the long-shoreman and then he turned to wave to their friends.

A few minutes later, Zorida and Das joined the fleeing pair in the great escape. Das and Conrad the coast guard slipped Okay a coast guard hat. They descended the various decks until they came to the main one where hundreds of people were still arriving.

"You need to stand up on your back legs," Zorida told Okay.

"Walk like a man," chimed Das.

Larry and Conrad, who had put their jobs and reputations on the line, urged Okay to put on the uniform. "Put your front feet in your pockets and walk between us." As Okay moved from his friends to the group of seamen, he was transformed into a dapper coast guard. Das and Zorida looked sadly at Okay. With the okapi in uniform, they didn't look like triplets any more. But they were able to move through the merrymakers without suspicion. In fact, Okay was greeted with salutes from others in uniform as they fled.

After wading through throngs of guests, they finally reached the rear docks where Okay turned to his good friends and told them, "You all have treated me like one of your own. I am sad to say goodbye and farewell."

Larry and Conrad were preparing to mount a small craft

they had waiting at the rear dock that would take them to the cargo ship bound for Africa. Sadly, Das and Zorida bid their friend a farewell.

Okay, Larry and Conrad boarded the small vessel. "Wait, wait, friends," said Okay, as he pulled off his distinctive coat made by Gianini the tailor. "Take this coat to remember our fun times together. I won't need it in Africa. The hat will be my keepsake. Soon I'll be home in the Wamba telling all the animals on the forest floor about my human friends, Harlem U.S.A. and my two great escapes."

Okay thought of his home nestled underneath the bamboo in the twinkling shiny light of day and the moonlight beams of night. He longed for the shadows of freedom where he could be wild. He could not wait to bathe and drink from the Ipulu water-falls. Soon he would munch on faso and dolea.

Das and Zorida laughed and cried as the craft sped away. On the little vessel, Okay laughed and cried too.

Das and Zorida watched as Okay and his top hat darted in and out of darkness. For an instant, the two caught a final glimpse of Okay aboard the cargo ship bound for Africa. Then it soon disappeared into the cloak of night.

Squirrel Paradise

by Myra Ndanu Consuela

THE SQUIRREL DARTED along the edge of the railing looking cautiously for any morsel left behind by his zoo neighbors.
The terrain was very familiar to him; he had lived his whole life
in the radius of the zoo. This winter had been harsher than pre-
vious ones. Although it was now May, the weather was cold and
the ground was still very hard. He had already dug up the last
remains of his winter food supply, which he had carefully buried
the year before. His sensitive nose had rooted out the nuts and
seeds he had buried along the small plots of land surrounding the
captive animals. Any food he had missed had already been dug
up by his fellow squirrels in the zoo who were also feeling the
strong pangs of hunger. He had fought to protect his stash but the
scarcity of food had driven them to dig up his territory—and
everywhere else—looking for something to eat. Now his hunger
was forcing him to visit his neighbors confined in the zoo.

Living within the comforts of the zoo environment, the
squirrel was not accustomed to struggling for every meal. During
the summer he depended on the good will of the visitors who
streamed through the zoo, passing him by to see the more interesting animals locked behind walls, moats and iron gates. He
didn't mind that they ignored him because they always left a
trail of food behind them. This spring, however, the cold rainy
weather had left the zoo empty. Most of the animals were inside,

along with their food supply. At times he could slip in and out of their open enclosures, stealing food at will.

Then there were other ways of getting food. Earlier in the winter season, a little white-haired lady would appear with a bag full of breadcrumbs and seeds. Her intention was to help the birds make it through the harsh winter. Since he did not know, or particularly care that this was not put there for him, he would race over to enjoy the small treats when the old lady threw out her crumbs. Sometimes she would shoo him with her cane and try to chase him away. This did not deter him. He would wait until she left to reappear and claim his meal. He looked forward to chasing the birds and enjoyed their treats with relish. He loved a good hunt for tasty nuts, but if he could not find a good nut, then bird treats were fine enough. However, it had been many weeks since the little lady had visited. The weather had kept her away and put an end to those meals.

As he walked along the edge of the zoo railing, a patch of green caught his attention. Just a few days ago the area had been a bare landscape. He'd heard the machinery and the loud voices of the workers, but he hadn't investigated that section for a while. The noise kept him away. Now the area looked green and very inviting. He decided to go down and investigate, so he moved agilely down the steep incline, and landed on a soft patch of grass.

In contrast to the bareness of some parts of the zoo, this place looked like a paradise. There was a soft covering of green and a large tree. At first he moved cautiously, examining the grounds and the patches of green grass. He also knew, since he had watched the workers dig up the area with bulldozers and trucks, that the humans always left something behind that he could eat. He moved around the space, sniffing and tasting the sprouts of grass. Then he noticed a parcel crumpled beside the tree. Sure enough, it was the remains of some food left behind by one of the workers. He greedily ate his find and then continued to look for more. "This is good," he thought, "if only I could find some more." He knew humans always left mounds of trash and he was not about to give up. There had to be more food.

As he moved away from the tree, a large hollow log caught his eye, so he went inside to investigate. His curiosity kept him from noticing the strange smell emanating from the area. A smell like that on any other occasion would have alerted him to danger, but he had become very relaxed about this place. He explored the log and was thinking it might be an excellent storage place for next winter's supply of nuts. So engrossed was he in his new found endeavors, that he didn't notice the yellow piercing eyes that were watching him or the huge yellow striped body that lay next to the log. Unaware, he sauntered out of the log ready to find the next meal in his newfound habitat.

As he emerged, he suddenly felt a ripping sensation across his back. His instincts told him to run, but when he tried, he felt another gripping sensation on his tail. He turned his head and realized, he was caught by the biggest cat he had ever encountered. The tiger toyed with him, letting him think he could get away, and then pounced on him again. The pain was excruciating, but each time he tried to get away, he was pulled back. The scent of his blood was everywhere and he was getting weaker and weaker. His senses began to fail him. Everything became a blur. Finally he gave up trying to escape. He knew this was the end. He was going to die and no one would care, not even his fellow squirrels. His death would mean one less squirrel to compete with. The birds definitely wouldn't miss him, as for the humans; well there was no comparing him to the magnificent creatures that inhabited the zoo. He was just another squirrel, at most a nuisance. He lay there limp.

Suddenly the tiger lost interest in his prey. His meal had arrived and he was more interested in the big chunks of raw meat laid out on stakes. When the squirrel awoke he did not remember climbing into the log, but that is where he found himself, too weak to move. He lay there in a pool of blood, scarcely breathing. The place that once looked like a paradise now seemed like a cage. He felt trapped.

He had always watched the other animals confined in their small quarters and appreciated the fact that he could dart from one area to another without notice. He had instinctively known which area was safe to invade and when to stay away. But his hunger had blinded him to danger. Now he was paying the ultimate cost for his mistake. Was he going to die? He didn't know how long he could live in this situation.

Since the log provided protection for him, he slept for hours but it seemed like days to him. When he woke up, he was very weak. The next day, his strength began to return to him and he started moving around the small space. But fear kept him from leaving the shelter and protection of the log. He had no idea what was happening outside.

Soon he realized that his fear was justified. He saw the menacing yellow eyes piercing through the opening in the log. Next, he felt the movement of the log as it was being pushed around. He dug his claws in the old wood in spite of the pain. The tiger was again toying with him. He could hear the scratching of the large paws on the outside of the log.

Again he saw the menacing eyes glaring at him through the opening. This went on for what seemed like an eternity. Finally it became quiet again, too quiet. The squirrel knew he would not be safe in the log forever. He had to escape.

He waited until the strange scent no longer filled his nostrils. He peeked his head out several times before he decided to make a break for it. Then he dashed through the patches of grass. The lush smell of the green was no longer inviting to him. Fear swelled his whole body. He reached the wall and immediately tried to scale it. His first attempt failed, but the second time he dug in and pulled himself up slowly. Luck was with him because the tiger was not in pursuit.

When he reached the top, he noticed the sun was out and there was a soft, warm breeze blowing. He raced past the sign reading, "Welcome to the Opening of Tiger Paradise! See these magnificent creatures in their natural habitat." He moved quickly past the crowd of people and the flashing cameras. He did not notice them or wonder if they had any food to leave him. He was heading toward familiar ground—somewhere he could feel safe. The crowd was too awed by the presence of "these magnificent creatures" to notice a squirrel racing by, not even one who had just escaped the jaws of a tiger and had lived to tell the story.

Saving Kenya Kesi

by Victoria Johnson

KESI LIFTED HER head from the acacia bush she was chewing and sniffed the warm evening breeze blowing over the golden grasslands of Kenya. Her sense of smell was very acute, as was her hearing, but her eyesight was poor. Therefore she relied heavily upon her allies, the birds. The yellow-crested oxpeckers, roosting on her back pecked at the bugs nesting in her mud-encrusted skin. They would warn her of impending danger if they took flight, but as they continued to peck and roost she felt confident in resuming her grazing. She thought she perceived a faint scent of man, but decided she was mistaken and again began to methodically pull leaves from the scrubby green brush.

Kesi was a young, black rhinoceros living in the shadow of the Aberdare Mountains of central Kenya. For millions of years, many species of rhinos roamed over Africa and Asia; now there were only five, three in Asia and the black and white rhinos of Africa, both in serious danger of becoming extinct. Kesi was a youngster at a year-and-a-half, weighing about a thousand pounds, and needed to consume more than the average rhino her

Sipho	(Cee-foh)
Kinara	(Kee-nah-rah)
jambiya	(jahm-bee-yah)
Kesi	(Keh-cee)
Hasina	(Hah-cee-nah)
Bakari	(Bah-kah-ree)
Odinga	(Oh-deen-gah)
Matiba	(Mah-tee-bah)

age. She was weaned from her mother by a force of circumstance only a few short months before, a full year earlier than most rhino calves. When her mother became a victim of poachers, Kesi was saved by a twist of fate. At the same moment the shots rang out mortally wounding her mother, a lion sprang from the bush to attack an antelope, which had wandered a short distance from its herd. During the ensuing confusion both Kesi and the lion managed to escape into the bordering leafy forest. Trying to bring down the lion and the young rhino, the shooting continued, but the bullets only ricocheted harmlessly off the surrounding trees.

Later, when all was quiet, Kesi returned. The serene grassland where she once grazed under her mother's watchful eye was now filled with overpowering and highly unpleasant smells as she found what was left of her mother's mangled and bloody body. A gaping wound was on the head which used to nuzzle her, where the cow's long and elegant horn had been chopped away. Kesi nudged her mother several times trying to rouse her. Finally realizing it was futile, she let out a long, forlorn wail. She cried because she didn't understand what was happening and was alone and afraid.

A nocturnal animal, Kesi spent the first night and day of her orphaned life in the shelter of the brush near her mother's carcass, eating little. Eventually hunger motivated her to wander forlornly through the bush the next night searching for food. After a while, she came upon another rhino cow and calf, managing to convince them that she belonged to their family. She wasn't allowed to nurse but was given the protection of the elder matriarch and Kesi was just old enough to find the food she needed to survive. But there were times when she would let out a high pitched cry, longing for the warmth of her mother's milk, more to satisfy their missing bond than to fill the hole created by any emptiness in her belly. Eventually she became more resigned to the absence of her mother and concentrated merely on staying alive.

As Kesi bent her head to pull off another branch of bush, Sipho Kinsaka, a young Bantu boy, slowly let out his breath. He thought for a moment that he and his friend, Kinara, had been spotted. Although a year younger than Kinara, his fourteen-year-old body was taller and more gangly. It was a lot harder for him to hide as the two of them hunched down beneath a clump of ragweed brush. For the last three years he had taken trips into the African bush, often with his schoolmate and friend, Kinara Odinga, to observe the wildlife his father was always talking about. His father, Bakari, worked for the Kenya Wildlife Service as the supervising ranger of the Aberdare National Park. He traveled hundreds of square miles of the bushland, searching for the elusive and treacherous poachers of elephants, rhinos, leopards and other endangered animals. There were times when Sipho was gravely concerned for his father's welfare, for his job was a very dangerous one.

Sipho first encountered the baby black rhino when he got the rare opportunity to fly with his father in the single helicopter, which the rangers used to canvas the vast territories of the park. The route he took after school lead him directly past the ranger's headquarters. One day as he headed toward home and his chores his father stepped out, calling to him, "Hey Sipho, you've saved me the task of coming to find you. How'd you like to take a helicopter ride with me?"

Sipho couldn't believe his ears. "Wow, you really mean it?"

"I sure do! I am going to be taking a scouting party into the bush in the next week or so and I thought before we leave it would be good to check the area by air. We have an extra seat and I thought you might like to come with us since you're out of school now."

"You bet I would!" Sipho was so excited he could barely contain himself. "Are we leaving now?"

"Just as soon as you get your mother's permission to skip your chores today."

"I'll be right back," cried Sipho as he hurried toward their house.

When he returned to ranger headquarters the helicopter was ready to go, its blades spinning lightly, causing little whirls of dust to spurt from the perimeter. Bakari grabbed Sipho's shoulder and pulled him toward the black and orange chopper. As they climbed in and got settled Sipho was handed a set of headphones, which would allow them to talk in spite of the noise from the helicopter. Suddenly the pilot started working the controls, the noise from the blades increased and the chopper rose from the ground in one swift motion. Sipho felt a bit giddy as he watched the ground recede and they began climbing through the sky. What a feeling! It was like nothing he had ever experienced before. He was filled with awe as the buildings of the village became smaller and smaller and he saw a seemingly endless expanse of the African bushland stretching toward the Aberdare Mountains in the far distance.

For about twenty minutes or so they cruised at an altitude that allowed them to view the land below without disturbing the grazing herds of elephants and wildebeests. Then they spotted a flock of vultures. As they flew in closer, Sipho could see that they were pecking at the carcass of a mutilated and bloated rhinoceros. It had been lying for several days in the hot African sun with the ants and termites eating at the wound created where the horn had been hacked away. These were the remains of Kesi's mother. The helicopter gently settled down near the dead rhino, causing the vultures to scatter.

When they disembarked and stood reviewing the carnage

there, Bakari commented sadly to his son, "That's a perfect example of greed, Sipho. The only thing of value that rhino had to offer those poachers was her horn. Although it's only made of keratin, the same thing our fingernails are made of, they prize her horn like it was made of gold."

"But why do they want the horns so much, Baba, Father?" Sipho asked.

"Many people in Asia think the powdered horn can cure illness and fever, even though aspirin works far better," his father replied. "There are also many who believe that a cup made from the horn protects them from poison. This makes it valuable to those who come to power by treachery."

Sipho was shocked. "That can't be the only reasons they want the horn, can it?" Sipho asked incredulously.

"No, unfortunately. Those factors would be relatively easy to fight against. The biggest market is in Yemen. When it's polished, the horn turns a beautiful, clear amber color and is used to make traditional *jambiya* dagger handles. Yemenites consider these daggers a symbol of manhood. In the past they were handed down through generations and usually available only to the aristocracy," Bakari explained. "The oil boom in Saudi Arabia in the 1970's created many jobs for Yemenites. When this happened they had more cash than they'd ever known before. The demand for *jambiya* began to skyrocket, creating a huge black market for rhino horns. There's a lot of people working to create a market of substitutes for these handles, but it'll be a while before the slaughtering is going to stop."

Sipho was astonished. "I can't believe people would risk wiping out an entire animal population just to make knife handles, Baba."

"Well, you'd better believe it, because it most certainly is happening. Men do some really stupid things sometimes," Bakari stated. He sighed and said, "You'd think they'd be smarter."

After the discovery of the carcass of the dead rhino, the helicopter scouted the entire area and Sipho, looking intensely over the dull green scrub brush suddenly cried out and pointed, "Look, Father, over there, to the right of that tree. There are some more rhinos."

What Sipho's sharp eyes had discovered in the low-lying brush was the unusual grouping of a mother rhino with two calves. It was obvious that the mother favored one of the calves over the other.

Bakari turned at Sipho's prompt, "Will you look at that. It seems like the dead rhino's calf managed to escape."

"Aren't they brother and sister, Father?" enquired Sipho.

"No Sipho, they're too close in age and rhino twins are extremely rare. I think that it is more likely this cow adopted the calf."

Sipho felt an immediate compassion for the young rhino. He didn't really understand why. Maybe it was because she looked so forlorn, standing just to the side of the large rhino cow and the favored calf. Mentally Sipho nicknamed her Kesi, which is Swahili for "one born during difficult times."

Since that day Sipho followed the growth of the young orphan calf. On afternoons when he was free from school assignments or work around the rangers' camp community, Sipho would run the several miles to the range that had been staked out as Kesi's territory, sometimes with his friend, Kinara, but often alone. He felt a sense of responsibility toward the young calf, perhaps because he felt helpless to stop the slaughter of the black rhinos. He hoped his father would be able to arrange for Kesi to be captured and sent to Lake Nakuru sanctuary.

A section of Lake Nakuru National Park had been fenced in to create a sanctuary, not to keep the wildlife in, but to assist in keeping poachers out. The black rhino had a greater likelihood of breeding when living in this region of Kenya. There, Kesi would have a fighting chance to grow up and have babies, adding to the dwindling black rhino population, currently in crisis.

Black rhinos in Kenya numbered about four hundred and each rhino calf born was crucially important. Although a sanctuary might be only as large as 15,000 acres, the rangers could guard it against the constant threat of poachers, unlike the vast expanses of the eastern African savannahs.

When Sipho returned to the Ranger's village that night he started in on Bakari again. "Baba, have you heard from the people at Lake Nakuru yet?"

Bakari looked down at his son's dark face with understanding eyes and replied, "I know you're concerned about your little rhino friend, Sipho, but there's nothing I can do until I get the go ahead from Thomas Kunene at Nakuru. He's pretty sure that he can get funding for the relocation but I probably won't hear from him until I return from this next patrol. I wish we could relocate her adoptive mother and brother, but, as funds are scarce, we have to pick the ones most likely to add to the gene pool and Kesi is 'it'. As soon as Thomas gives me permission we'll move Kesi to the sanctuary, but until then my hands are tied."

Sipho tried not to look too disappointed. He didn't want to make things any harder than necessary for his father. The patrol his father referred to was tedious and dangerous, but of the utmost importance. A party of six to eight rangers would ride out on camels into the dry African savannah and into the forests of the Aberdare Mountains for a week or so, looking for poachers. They often found the illegal hunters with bloody outcomes. The rangers, armed only with single-action rifles, were unequally matched with the highly dangerous poachers, who carried automatic weapons. Their only connection to the village at these times was by radio. Sipho had every reason to be concerned.

The next morning as the sun was beginning to lighten the eastern sky, Sipho, his mother, grandmother, and two little sisters, along with many others in their camp village, waved farewell to the small troop of rangers as they departed into the brush. When the convoy disappeared into the shimmering haze of growing sunlight, the onlookers drifted off to their various tasks. Sipho sighed as he took one last look and led his sisters toward the white stucco schoolhouse in the center of the village. He resolved to run out to the bush after school and check on Kesi. He worried that something would happen to the young rhino before his father returned. Sipho didn't know just what he could do, but at least he could be assured that she was safe for the moment.

When Sipho returned home that day after school it turned out his mother, Hasina, had different ideas about how he should be spending his time.

"Sipho, I need you to watch your little sisters while I go to the market," his mother told him. "And your grandmother says there are far too many weeds in the garden. Please take care of it while I'm out."

"But Mama, I was going to go and check on Kesi today," Sipho cried.

"Not today, you're not. I need your help at home. Besides, what do you think you are going to be able to do for her before your father hears from Lake Nakuru?"

"I don't know, but at least I would know that she's safe today," Sipho replied.

"That might be true, but you will just have to hope that she will be kept safe for you." Hasina, having made this statement, turned and left. Sipho sighed and, letting his little sisters know that he didn't want any trouble from them, went out to weed their garden.

The next several days, whenever he got a break from a seemingly endless amount of schoolwork, his mother or grandmother managed to find another chore for him to do. Finally, after a few days Hasina relented and told him that he could have the afternoon off after school and have some free time with his friends. During the lunch break at school that day Sipho pulled Kinara aside, "Kinara, my mother's finally letting me off this afternoon. Can you come with me into the bush to check on Kesi?"

Kinara grinned, "You sure do have it bad for that rhino calf. Are you going to single-handedly take on all the poachers in Kenya to keep her safe?" He laughed and said, "Okay, I'll go with you. My mother's preoccupied with her sister's new child right now. Anyway, I don't think she'll miss me much."

That afternoon, immediately after school, Sipho and Kinara headed toward the lake where Sipho had last seen Kesi. They made a short trip of it as they ran down the dusty dirt road, clowning and horsing around with the bright spirits of the young freed from responsibility on a hot and sunny day. As they approached the lake, Kinara pointed at a group of rocks and commented, "If we climb to the top of those we might be able to see Kesi." It was only a matter of minutes after they mounted their lookout when they spotted the group of three rhinos not far from the lake, chewing on some acacia trees.

"Now we know where they are, let's see if we can get closer," Sipho said.

"But why?" asked Kinara. "You already know they're safe at the moment."

"Sure I do. But I still want to get closer. Unless, of course, you don't think you are enough of a hunter to get any closer to your prey," Sipho said with a teasing voice.

Kinara sighed and replied, "One of these days you should

capture this rhino and bring it home to be the family pet."

Sipho just laughed and said, "Let's go then."

They clambered down from their rocky perch and headed in the direction of the lake where the rhinos were feeding. As they approached, Sipho and Kinara got very quiet, finally dropping to all fours as they came into the acacia grove. As stealthily as predatory cats they noiselessly crawled under the bushes, making sure they were down wind so as not to alert their visual prey. Finally they were able to see the three rhinos as they grazed, the cow sticking much closer to her calf with Kesi being noticeably smaller. At one point Sipho thought that they had been spotted as Kesi stopped eating suddenly and raised her head, listening intently. After a few minutes, however, she decided that there was no need for alarm and resumed feeding. Sipho let out a low sigh of relief and realized that he had been holding his breath.

They had been in position for several minutes when Kinara felt something on his leg. Turning he saw a beetle with long pincers resting on the back of his knee. He jumped and yelled. This, of course, immediately set off a chain reaction. The rhinos jerked their heads to attention and wasted no time running off in the opposite direction. Sipho grabbed a stick and knocked the beetle off Kinara in one fluid motion.

Then he started to laugh. "Boy, you need to practice some more if you're going to be a tracker some day. Scared of a little beetle?"

Kinara grinned sheepishly. "Yeah, well I noticed you didn't use your hand to knock it away. That stick was awfully convenient. Anyway, it's time we headed back."

The sun was beginning its slow glide toward the horizon as they came to the village. This was usually a time of relaxed and quiet activity in the settlement as lights began to pop on in the houses and the smell of cooking permeated the air as dinners were prepared. But things were decidedly different this evening. Many people were outside their houses talking in excited voices. When they saw Sipho and Kinara the talking stopped abruptly and one of Sipho's cousins, Mosi, spoke to him, "Your father's back, Sipho. He's looking for you two. You and Kinara should go to the ranger station immediately." Mosi gave Kinara a swift but odd, sideways glance.

Sipho looked at Kinara puzzled. "The scouting party wasn't due back this soon. Are you sure?"

"Just go to the station," was the reply.

Sipho shrugged, clearly perplexed, and headed to the place he knew as his second home. When they arrived there was a large group of rangers milling around the entrance of the station, speaking in low tones. The boys could tell that something serious was happening.

Bakari was there and called to Sipho and Kinara, directing them into his office. He was so grave looking that Sipho was afraid. Did they do something wrong? Should they not have gone into the bush today? After they were seated Bakari cleared his throat and stated solemnly, "There is no way to make this easier, Kinara. This morning we confronted a group of poachers trying to massacre an elephant herd. We succeeded in saving most of the herd but unfortunately one ranger and one poacher were killed. The ranger was your father, Kinara. I am so sorry."

Sipho could not believe his ears. He looked at Kinara, who sat there looking stunned. Finally Kinara choked out, "You're sure?"

Bakari nodded and said, "I wish I could say I wasn't. Let me take you home to your mother, now. She is going to need you."

Bakari put his arm around Kinara and turned to his son, "Sipho, your mother and grandmother are with Kareem's wife. I don't want her to be alone right now. Can I count on you to get your sisters fed and in bed?"

Sipho, very shocked by the news, replied to his father, "Of course, Baba. I'll do whatever I can to help."

As Bakari and Kinara left for the Odinga home Sipho tried to marshal his sisters through dinner and the bedtime routine. Although his thoughts were racing they were also confused, going nowhere fast. Sipho didn't know what he could say to his friend.

That night as he lay sleepless in his bed he heard his father and mother return. He listened to the low tones of his parents conversing when his father suddenly cried, "What is more important, the life of an animal or the life of a human being? I don't know the answer." Bakari sounded tired and confused. Sipho was not used to hearing his father sound powerless and it made him uneasy.

The following day, after Kareem's burial, Sipho approached Kinara and tried to stammer out how badly he felt. Kinara had already heard from many people and was very tired of reliving it over and over again. When Sipho, his friend, came to speak with him, it was like a dam suddenly burst, allowing him to talk freely, "I know, I know. Everyone is so sorry."

"It must be hard, Kinara." Sipho wished he knew how to console his friend. "Do you have any idea of what you and your family are going to do now?"

"My mother is worried that I am going to follow in my relative's footsteps."

"Which relative? Is he a bad man?" Sipho asked, puzzled.

"My father's cousin has been a poacher for years. In one month, without poaching, he makes maybe twenty U.S. dollars, when he poaches, he earns as much as one-hundred-fifty U.S. dollars an animal. What is a poor man to do? I don't want to shame my father and the work that he did, but now I need money to support my family!" Kinara broke down, crying. "What am *I* supposed to do?" Sipho didn't know what to say to his friend.

That afternoon Bakari informed his family he would have to return to the bush and the scouting party, which had stayed behind, looking for the remaining poachers. Sipho knew his father was working to save their heritage and African wildlife and he was proud of his determination and bravery. But now he was all too aware that the danger his father faced was very real. He tried not to be worried, but he was afraid that his father might be the next victim.

When Sipho awoke the next day Bakari was already gone. His mother told him that she would be with the Odingas when he returned from school and to just make sure that his chores and homework were done. It was rare that Sipho deliberately disobeyed his parents, but he saw this as a chance to check on Kesi. That afternoon as the blue and white uniformed children noisily poured through the doors of the schoolhouse, Sipho held back, filling his canteen at the water spigot on the side of the building. When things became relatively quiet he headed toward the bush range which Kesi and her adopted family roamed. As Sipho trotted further out into the open savannah he looked around, breathing in the beauty of the untouched land. The sky was a vast bowl of intense blue, the rim resting on the top of the Aberdare Mountains in the distance. A steady but gentle breeze caused the grasses to undulate like silent waves with no shore to break them. There was a dry, fresh scent that made Sipho want to breathe to the very bottom of his lungs. A half-mile away he could see a small herd of giraffe stretching their necks, gracefully pulling the leaves from a baobab tree. Further east, near a small lake, a herd of gray elephants could be seen relaxing in the water, spraying each other with their immense trunks.

As Sipho watched the shenanigans of the elephant party,

several things happened almost simultaneously. Three shots rang out, shattering the peaceful tableau, causing a flock of sunbirds to lift from the surface of the lake as a unit and fly away. The giraffes began running with immense strides and Sipho could feel the earth vibrate under his feet as the lumbering elephants rose and began to scatter. Three of the herd stumbled along for several steps and, as more shots were heard, they slowly fell to the ground, to move no more.

Sipho watched, horrified, as a group of men rose from the brush and walked toward the fallen animals. He was too far away to hear what they were saying or to clearly see what they were doing, but then, he really didn't need to be there. He knew he had just witnessed poachers in action, taking down elephants for their ivory tusks, another valuable commodity in the black market. Although he wanted to get closer to identify the poachers later, he dared not. He was aware that it was worth his very life to try something like that. The fact that he was unarmed and alone made him no match for the dangerous and desperate men.

Sipho was sickened at the thought of what took place and frustrated because there was literally nothing he could do to stop it. The only option he had now was to inform the rangers, so he started back to the village. Since the poachers were still in the immediate area he didn't know if they might be tracking Kesi. Filled with anxiety, he hoped the rangers on duty in the village could alert his father's patrol or send out more rangers to discourage the poachers, maybe keeping the rhinos safe until word came from Lake Nakuru.

As Sipho hurried through the brush, the trees began to transform into black silhouettes, in sharp contrast to the orange and gold sky of the setting sun. The noisy chatter of the monkeys began to taper off. Sipho trudged along and considered the dilemmas that faced both the animals and the poachers. He, himself, didn't always know what to do. God would have to guide him as he tried to help his friend, Kinara, and the orphan Kesi.

When he finally got to the village he ran to the ranger station to find Lt. Matiba, the senior ranger in his father's absence, sitting at his desk going through paperwork under the soft glow of a lamp. Lt. Matiba looked up as Sipho burst through the door out of breath. A tired smile lit his round brown face. "Hello, Sipho! I have good news for you. I received a letter today from the people at Lake Nakuru. They've given us permission to capture your little rhino friend and ship her to their sanctuary as soon as the patrol returns."

As soon as he spoke Lt. Matiba became aware that Sipho was very upset and agitated.

"What's wrong, Sipho?" he asked, his tired eyes quickly registering his concern. Sipho could not reply immediately as he was out of breath from running. As soon as he could he began to gasp out, "Poachers…out near the lake…have killed…elephants."

Lt. Matiba rose and hurried to pour some water for Sipho. Handing him the glass he said, "Drink this, catch your breath and then tell me what you saw."

Sipho followed the Lt.'s advice and as his breathing slowed, he relayed what he had just witnessed to the ranger. As he finished he blurted out, "Lt. Matiba, the news about Lake Nakuru is great, but how can we keep Father and Kesi safe until the patrol returns?"

"Your father is relatively easy. I will radio him immediately. As for Kesi, well, we can only try," Lt. Matiba replied. "I will get some rangers and go investigate the area tomorrow. Your father should return the day after tomorrow and we'll start the move then. Try not to worry."

That was going to be easier said than done, Sipho thought, as he said goodnight to Lt. Matiba, but he didn't have much choice. The next day after school he headed straight for the station to get the latest news. Lt. Matiba and his rangers had just returned from the bush. Sipho didn't have to say a word, the anxious, questioning expression on his face spoke volumes.

"We found the elephants, Sipho, but there doesn't seem to be any sign of harm toward your rhinos, though we did find signs they had been grazing in the area recently. I radioed your father again and he said that he should be back by midday tomorrow. We'll find them then and begin the relocation process the following morning. Until then, we'll just have to hope for the best."

Sipho could barely contain his anxiety and excitement. He would be sorry to see Kesi leave but he knew that it was the best thing possible for her. That night and the next day seemed to take a hundred years to pass. When the school bell rang it was as if Sipho had been shocked by a jolt of electricity the way he jumped up from his desk and headed for the door. He went in search of his father and found that Bakari was already in the bush, tracking the rhinos. Sipho had to be content returning home, to wait in agony while he completed his schoolwork and chores.

As the evening shadows grew longer, Sipho, trying to concentrate without success on his homework, simply gazed out the window. When he spotted Bakari coming down the dusty road, Sipho jumped up to open the door, crying out, "Father, did you find them?"

Bakari laughed and said, "What—no hello for the weary traveler?"

Sipho looked abashed and started to stammer but Bakari cut him off. "Don't worry, son. I know how concerned you've been. I found their current grazing range but didn't see any more signs of the poachers. Maybe they've left the area. I certainly hope so. The rhinos shouldn't travel too far tonight. I've contacted Dr.

Sherman and we'll go out and start Kesi's move tomorrow morning at first light."

Dr. John Sherman was a local research scientist, studying and documenting many species of wildlife in the Aberdares. Although a white man, he was a native Kenyan, educated in veterinary science in England, and was passionate about saving as much of Kenya's natural resources as possible. He was responsible for researching the endangered species of Kenya, which included the rhinoceros.

Bakari gave his son a quick hug and said, "With a little luck Kesi should be on her way to Lake Nakuru by afternoon. Since tomorrow is Saturday, would you like to come with us? You'd have to stay in the back, but you could be a part of the move."

Sipho felt a sense of relief that was almost physical, followed by a giddy feeling of excitement at the thought of working with the rangers. He nodded eagerly to his father and choked out, "You bet!"

The next morning Sipho and Bakari were up long before the sun, when the birds were just beginning to call to each other from the trees. The monkeys were waking, swinging from the branches, chattering noisily as the men from the animal rescue team began assembling at the ranger station. Their party consisted of five rangers, six assistants, Dr. Sherman, the vet, and Sipho. They were to take the trip into the African bush in the ranger's camouflaged jeep and a large truck to transport Kesi to Lake Nakuru.

By the time they finally started out for the bush it was full daylight. Sipho got to ride in the jeep with his father and Dr. Sherman. As they bounced along the faint trails that passed for roads Bakari commented to the others in the vehicle, "It's going to take about a half hour to reach the edge of the rhino's grazing range. When we get to that point we'll have to send some trackers in by foot to locate their exact position. They'll back off and radio the specs to you, Dr. Sherman. Then you'll get to go in and work your magic."

Dr. Sherman laughed, "Twentieth-century magic." He turned his interest toward Sipho, fixed his intent gaze on him and stated, "So you've taken an interest in African wildlife, have you?"

Sipho nodded shyly. "It seems like there's a need to protect so many animals and Father always says there is not enough men or money to do the kind of job he would like."

"Well, your father's a smart man and absolutely right. But we're making progress. A few years ago the rhino was almost extinct. In Kenya alone there were only about twenty animals and not many more than that in other countries. But with a lot of hard work combined with the creation of sanctuaries and breeding programs, they now number in the hundreds. It would be a shame if the only way your children could see animals like rhinos, elephants and leopards was on video or as illustrations in a picture book." Dr. Sherman said encouragingly, "I hope you continue your interest. We can always use another good man like your father."

Sipho liked what the doctor said and tried to think of a good response. His attention was distracted though when Bakari pulled the jeep under a large acacia tree and stopped. Bakari climbed out and walked over to the truck behind him. "This is as far as the vehicles go. It's your turn now," he told the trackers. Go find Sipho's girl friend before he worries himself to death over her." The trackers grinned and said they thought they could handle it. Sipho watched as they disappeared into the bush.

In a relatively short time the radio began to crackle. "Bakari, we've found the rhinos. They're sleeping now but have Dr. Sherman come cautiously." Dr. Sherman listened while the tracker proceeded to give his coordinates and directions.

Sipho watched while the doctor loaded a tranquilizer dart into his rifle. While doing this he explained just what was going to happen first. "This is a fast-acting tranquilizer, Sipho. It will take effect in a few seconds. When she is completely under I will give her another injection of antibiotics to keep any infection from starting."

Dr. Sherman looked at Sipho for a minute, then went over to Bakari and spoke softly with him. When he turned around he looked pleased and said nonchalantly, "Since you've come this far in helping Kesi, do you think you could keep from spooking the rhinos if you came with me on this last trek?"

Sipho was shocked and elated. This was so much more than he ever thought he would be able to do. He nodded eagerly, "If you let me come, I promise I won't make a sound."

They left for the bush together, walking silently for about ten minutes. Sipho watched while Dr. Sherman crept quietly within firing range of the small group of rhinos. The weathered lines around his bright blue eyes deepened as he took careful aim through the sight of his gun. He gently squeezed the trigger and Sipho heard a small pop. Kesi heaved slightly and lumbered forward, the oxpeckers on her back taking flight in alarm. She managed only a dozen paces or so before she stumbled and sank to her knees, falling over as the tranquilizer took effect. The cow and her calf ran into the surrounding bush, not knowing what had frightened them, but sensing it was better to put some distance behind them.

After this the trackers moved forward and found Kesi still conscious as they grouped around her, but this didn't last long. As Sipho approached, he saw her try to lift her head, which sank down again. Her eyes gradually closed and her labored breathing became steady and even. Dr. Sherman gave her the second injection and radioed for the vehicles to meet them.

Taking a gray quilted cotton mask from his bag, Dr. Sherman placed it over Kesi's face. Sipho, finally overcoming his initial shyness, asked, "What's that for?"

"Well, it's going to take several hours for her to be transported to Lake Nakuru. Even though she's tranquilized, there is always the possibility that she'll wake prematurely. If her eyes are covered she's less likely to get agitated and should remain calmer. Also, keeping the light away from her eyes will make it more likely that she'll stay under until the end of the trip."

"What'll happen when she gets there, Dr. Sherman?" Sipho wondered.

"It's going to take several weeks before she's actually released into the main part of the sanctuary. The immediate things that will happen are she'll be put in a small enclosure, the bindings will be removed and she'll be released into a temporary compound. She'll share the compound with a goat as a companion while she adjusts. A companion animal always seems to make the relocation a little easier."

After tying her legs together with a stout rope, the rangers and handlers began the hard work of getting the rhino pushed and rolled onto a large platform. The cool of the early morning was succumbing to the increasing heat of the day as the sun rose higher in the sky. Sweat glistened on the faces and bodies of the workers as they labored, hauling the young rhino up and into the back of the high-sided truck. Their spirits were light though as they joked back and forth. Bakari kidded them, "She's just a baby. This should be a piece of cake for you strong young men."

One of them grinned back and said, "Yeah, a thousand pound baby. Her daddy must've been on steroids."

Bakari laughed and gave another push to the litter.

Finally, Kesi was loaded onto the truck and the tailgate was closed and fastened behind her. As Sipho stood back and looked at her for the final time he knew that the recent object of his care and concern would be gone from his part of Kenya. However, having one more young and healthy rhino that could breed and add to the small but growing population of black rhinos was going to be of immense importance. His satisfaction with Kesi's future was dimmed at the thought of the price that was continually being paid to ensure the survival of these endangered animals. He could now understand the dilemma his father faced on a daily basis: which was more important, the life of a man or the animal?

Kesi was groggy when she woke. Her eyes opened and, though she knew things were different, she couldn't figure out what happened or where she was. She was in a small pen not much bigger than she was and the cow and her calf were gone. She was afraid and began to turn around, running at the wooden sides, trying to ram her way out to the grasslands she knew. There were men looking over the high sides of the pen, which frightened her further. Without warning a gate opened and she ran through into a larger area that looked much more familiar. It wasn't big but there were acacia bushes, a few trees, and grass covering the rest, but there was still no rhino cow and calf. Suddenly another creature was at her side, one she had never encountered before. It seemed determined to engage her, but not in a menacing manner. There were two stubby horns on its head with which it kept butting her in a playful manner, so it was hard to ignore. She hadn't played at anything in a while. Maybe this wasn't so bad after all.

Illustration by Cheryl Hanna

Brother to the Wolf

by Cheryl Hanna

EMMANUEL KING WAS a gentleman. Even under pressure, even though he had fallen on hard times, he had been and remained a gentleman. People recognized that, sometimes unwillingly.

On Monday, Emmanuel's routine took him first to the bagel shop on 145th and Amsterdam where his latest friend among the low-paid and harried teenage employees was saving a bag of day-old bagels for him. Emmanuel thanked God daily that he was still blessed with all his teeth. And then he thanked the muscular young lady behind the counter, who had a paper hat perched uncertainly on her short—whaddaya call 'em?—dreads and watched her face, sullen in repose, brighten into charm. You just know she get up every morning and curse out that paper hat. What was her name? Kalima? Emmanuel always took a minute and found out the names of the people he dealt with—his daddy taught him that—call people by they name.

Sure enough, after he called her by her name, Kalima put a couple fresh bagels in his bag. She didn't know he liked the stale ones. Well, he'd save them for company. Emmanuel thanked her again and went on his way puzzling over her smile. Who she remind him of? He was at an age when the whole human race seemed like it wanted to be an ocean, one that returned to the same shore time and again in rhythmic waves—

each and every wave proclaiming its uniqueness, its difference, before it crashed into the shore and was gone.

His brother Barry's first wife? That woman used to do hair on 136th Street, the one his wife used to go to? Emmanuel took a bagel out of the bag, gave it a small surreptitious bite. You weren't supposed to eat on the subway. Woman on the opposite seat gave him a glare. Kill people, pee in the corners, stretch out and sleep on the seats if you had to, but don't sneak a bite off a bagel. Woman just kept on glaring. Who she remind him of? Somebody evil. His boy Jerome's first school principal—the one who wanted to drug him silly? Woman in the dry cleaners that time they went and lost the suit he got married in? Emmanuel snuck another bite, lost interest. He was at an age when he was more than ready to let the evil folks go on about their business. Let 'em be. If they would just let him be.

He debated his next stop. On Monday, his routine gave him a choice at certain junctures. He could head on up to the zoo, visit with his brother wolf a little while, settle his mind for the week. Or he could go the other way and drop in at the library, get himself an old favorite or something with a shiny new cover, allow himself a rental book. Monday's routine only called for pleasant things— pleasures and privileges.

Tuesday, well, Tuesday he might have to put on a suit and a tie and go down to the electric to ask for an extension. Might as well stop in at the Social Security while he was at it and fin- ish ruining the day.

Emmanuel yanked his mind on back to Monday's choice of pleasures. Tuesday'll get here, he reminded himself. After the zoo or the library he could head on home to 156th Street and see if he could find a chess game in the pocket park in front of the buildings. Willie G. might be out there—Willie give him a good game. Or there was the little farmer's market Monday afternoons on 110th out in front of the shelter—Amish folks with fruit, pies, meat and vegetables. He could allow himself a taste or two. Must be some other bill he could pay late, or maybe split them yellow pills, the beta-something, in half for a week or so—that would save him fifteen dollars. He'd done it before and survived.

Emmanuel decided to head on up to the zoo and visit with the wolf a while, then go and see if he could find ole Mister Willie G.—Mr. William G. Tilly. Also known as Wild Bill. And Mister Till. And Billy Tilly. Depending who you talked to. Lunch could be a frankfurter from a street stand or maybe something off McDonald's dollar menu . . . and wasn't *that* a public service. Plus if he went to McDonald's he could stock up on dinner napkins.

Train up to the Bronx, people kept coming at him in waves. Boy cross the car look just like that friend his brother Barry had when he got out the army. Two big feet, three feet apart, hands in pockets, wanna see how much space he could take up. Another glare for him, black eyes challenging—*what chu lookin' at ole man?*

Emmanuel averted his eyes, smiling to himself. Look just like Barry's friend. He remembered being that age—restless— eager—hungry. Got his book out of the pocket of his old black overcoat. Emma Lee bought him that coat down at B. Altman's on Fifth Avenue, her favorite place to shop.

Mondays, Emmanuel read only for pleasure. Today, he was dipping into *Treasure Island*. Reading with two, maybe three minds. On top, an old man, one with a patchy gray beard— when it came in—and seamed cheeks, an old man the girls didn't look at. Underneath, a black-eyed boy, a restless boy, on a ship halfway around the world from home, the sea under him making him dip and roll like an ant on the palm of a giant striding across the world. Emmanuel missed the sea, that was one thing he gave up when he got himself married. God, he missed that dip and roll, that assurance, even sleeping, that he was on his way somewhere. Sweet Emma Lee! Powerful sweet woman to make a man give up the sea he loved and trade it in on a city still surprised him by going nowhere at all. 'Cept the people came in waves.

Emmanuel went back to his book. Underneath that boy on the ship, a country-born flatland child never seen the sea. Emmanuel smiled as he read, noticing again with his top mind how Stevenson left the women out the picture altogether. Still, there were hints. Long John's wife: a woman of color, a woman of the islands. As a child and a young man, Emmanuel would try and fail to imagine just what kind of woman would partner up with Long John—aid and abet his pirate schemes. Now, with the perspective of old age, looking down the long years, well, Emmanuel could just see her—somebody like that Louise—woman used to run the Caribbean bakery down the block from him and Emma Lee's first place. Emmanuel cackled to himself. Woman once threw a greasy bag of pasties at his head 'cause he asked if she was expecting. She wasn't. He shook his head, laughing at the memory. Yeah, ole Long John's wife was probably just like Louise. Ready to kill you or cure you—full of hate and love and ready to deal out both or either at a moment's notice.

But when Emma Lee was sick and he was out of work and broke, didn't she give them free food for a month? Didn't she give it so a proud man could take it? Didn't she? Emmanuel shook his head, remembering. But when that fool come in there looking to rob her, didn't she come out from behind that counter like a fury? Didn't she? Fool ran all the way down 110th screaming, tryin' to make out later she had a gun. Evil woman armed with a coupla cooking utensils. Emmanuel closed his eyes, finger in his book, leaning back, bagel bag in his lap, dreaming a little.

Thinking about Long John's woman and Louise from down the block, Emmanuel realized the waves were bigger than he knew. Not just crashing through one man's life like he thought, but washing down through the centuries and around the world. Hell, maybe someday out into outer space. Just another rolling sea for some lucky country boy, born long time after they buried him.

He woke with a start at his stop. Got out, followed a school group at what he hoped was a safe distance. Excited children, a harried teacher, a kind one. One little boy turned around and looked him dead in the face—big ole solemn dark eyes—and the wave struck him in the heart. Jerome's face.

"I'm goin' to see the lions," said the child, confidentially. His teacher—the nice one—saw him talking to a strange man and hurried over to gather him back into her flock. Pretty woman. She gave Emmanuel an apologetic smile. Emmanuel smiled back. Just doing her job. Bad people running about nowadays. Got to keep the little ones close. Teacher grabbing the child's arm, whispering warnings in his baby ear, but that little boy's face turnt around anyway and his eyes fastened on Emmanuel's. Father-hunger, Emmanuel recognized the signs. He sighed. He was old; too tired to be more than a granddaddy, but everywhere he looked seemed like he met young boys needing more. *On his way to see the lions . . .* He walked the rest of the way to the zoo ahead of the group of children, listening to the noise they made pulling up behind him, thinking about that little boy's face.

Emmanuel went to pay his eight dollars at the gate. Cashier wanted to see his card. Fool could look up and see she was dealing with an old man. Emmanuel grumbled, fumbling among his bags and pockets while a restless line formed behind him. Some smart-aleck teenagers started making fun of the things he pulled out of his pockets in his search. Just what was so funny about a pocketknife? And what's the kitchen can opener doin' in his pocket? Tall gangly boy had him a girl up under each arm, looking like he invented sliced bread and put the "p" in peanut butter. Can opener really tickled him. *Just you wait, youngblood,* Emmanuel promised him silently, *You ain't gon' be young forever.* Emmanuel been a tall boy hisself, but never silly enough to fool with more than one woman at time. His daddy used to say every ass can only ride one horse. Emmanuel snorted at the memory, still fumbling, while the line behind him went from restless to raucous. Somebody with some sense came up behind the cashier, trying to see what the hold up was, took one look at him, grabbed his money and waved him through. That girl woulda let him stand there looking for his card until that line turnt into a lynch mob. Like there were people running around here *pretending* to be old. Old age ain't Disneyland with folks begging to get in....

He took a roundabout way to the wolf habitat. Enjoying the new green, the little bit of chill in the air. Seem like some years the city went straight from way-too-cold to way-too-hot, no more than a breath of all-right between the seasons. Emmanuel never meant to grow old in the city. Him and Emma Lee had a nice little piece of property upstate. Outside a funny little town call itself Liberty, New York. They had plans to build. But he lost all that, Barry got himself in trouble and he spent everything they had trying to pull him out one last time.

Emmanuel got to the wolf habitat, sat down on the convenient bench, across the way, settled in, quiet, waiting on his brother wolf.

Emmanuel had been a farm boy, a sailor boy, a city man, but he never had much to do with wild things or with the knowledge of wild things. A year or two ago when he added the zoo to his routine, it had more to do with the senior citizen discount, the pleasant walks and handy benches, the sense of order and care that lay over the place—plus plenty of them guards. Got comfortable coming for other reasons, then the animals caught his attention. It was like a whole new world, a whole lot of interlocking worlds that he'd never paid any mind to.

Here come brother wolf up close to the moat at the edge of the habitat, sniffing and looking in on him. Emmanuel looked back. There was a noisy family in front of him, but he paid them no mind and the wolf paid them no mind. It was his wolf, not one of the others, not that he wasn't glad to see them too. He nodded at brother wolf and brother wolf greeted him back, before he turned to lope out to a further corner of the habitat, his gray dappled coat blending with the shadows, even in the sunlight. Wolf settling down there in the dappled shade of a clump of trees, wolf colored silver like a shadow at dawn. Another wolf peeked briefly out the den carved high in the man-made hill. Noisy family howled, threw a popcorn box, like that was going to tempt the wolves back. Guide came over to explain to them how to act. Emmanuel settled in to wait them out.

The thing the wolf put him in mind of, the thing he came out here to think on—was freedom. He hadn't seen much of it. Even if he hadn't been a black man in white man's America, he'd still been a son, a brother, a husband, a father. Started working when he was fourteen. That was as long as his own father could hold off the world. One job, two jobs, sometimes three jobs and then something on the side. Emmanuel shook his head, thinking how much of him and Emma Lee's life-savings they'd poured down the rat hole of Barry's last defense. Not that he wasn't guilty, 'cause he was. Emmanuel chuckled a little. Money he'd had. And people depending on him. And obligations. And responsibilities. And commitments. Now the question was—had he outlived them all and could he sit here in the sun and think, think at length on a wolf's yellow eyes and how they put him in mind of freedom?

Noisy family passed on. Maybe went to peek in the monkey house, see if they could learn some new tricks. Or walk around the corner, where they had a place cut into the man-made hill, you could look in the den, see the new spring cubs. Emmanuel had never been over there, aside from the fact he didn't like to spend the extra three dollars on top of general admission, he had a problem with the peeking in the wolf den. Might be educational and all, but didn't seem right. See the new cubs when they was ready to be seen, when they parents brought them into the sun.

Wolves stayed out hiding in the shadows. Emmanuel began to get a chill in his bones, started thinking on some lunch. After all, it was too cold to sit out here on a bench and eat. Go on home, drop off these packages, open a can of soup. Now here come the class with his friend, little father-hungry boy. Teacher had him by one hand, but he waved to Emmanuel with the other. Emmanuel waved back.

On the train downtown he sat back, closed his eyes, let a wave of weariness wash pass him, smiled to himself. After all, what he had now, it was a luxury wasn't it? By some standards, he was hard-up, peanut butter for dinner, library books in his duffel, paper bag stuffed full of day-old bagels, but Emmanuel counted himself rich. He had time to think. And his thoughts roamed free. Not like when he was making money—and he made a whole lot of money. All of it gone. What was a man made for if not to think? A man ain't a engine. A man ain't a machine.

Emmanuel gathered his hands into fists on his knees, forced himself to let go of the old anger. Decided to make the stop at the Amish market. What them folks have today? Must be a good way to live, your own land, your own way of doing things. Not the way he grew up, everything hardscrabble, couldn't wait to get out of there, then he fell in love with the sea. He dozed, dreaming of the ocean, missed his stop, had to double back and decided to go on home, do the market on Thursday.

At the door to his apartment, he hesitated, briefly confused. Who's waiting over there in the shadow where one corner runs into another and the light don't fall? Not one of them fool boys break in here before... Tall, narrow peanut head, those jitterbug shoulders, redbone complexion, yellow dog eyes. The wave hit him, swept him off his feet this time, he swayed over his bags and dropped his face into his hands. Barry... Boy ran forward and caught him by the elbows, steadied him with a murmur. "Watch it, Granddaddy," said the boy with his brother Barry's yellow dog eyes. "You alright?"

Emmanuel caught his breath, put his confusion away like an out-of-season overcoat, put things in their place. This was Barry's grandson. He was in New York City, in Harlem. Barry Redman King died in jail, disgracing his folks. Emma Lee King been dead for ten long years. Emmanuel Barefield King is an old man, he told himself fiercely, with thirty-two fifty to last him until next Monday, not counting bottle deposits and what he might pick up in the park playing chess—if he could find somebody to play didn't know him.

"Granddaddy?" asked the boy, anxiously. Emmanuel realized he hadn't spoken out loud. Well, that was good. He believed in casting a veil over the infirmities of old age.

"I'm alright, let go of me." Couldn't remember the boy's name for a minute, still confusing him with his brother Barry, then that fell into place too, "Akinde, here, he'p me with these bags." Boy didn't have to be asked twice. Emmanuel twisted the keys in his three stiff locks, considering how two people as careless and confused as this boy's parents came to settle on just the right name for him. Proper African name.

Emmanuel eased into his favorite chair, still in his coat. Akinde brought him a glass of tap water. Emmanuel drank it down, noticing it was clear. Akinde'd let the tap run. One good thing, you didn't have to tell him twice. Quiet—too quiet, watchful, careful—too careful. Emmanuel offered him lunch. Look at him considering the offer from all the angles. Thinking it over. Did he want some lunch? Maybe he didn't? Would he have to cook it? What's on the menu? What's he getting into?

"Okay," Akinde told him, finally. Then stood there waiting for the other shoe to drop. Emmanuel resisted the temptation to tease him. He could use a little fun, but he wasn't sure that was what the boy needed.

In the kitchen, he groaned a little, shrugging out of his coat and hanging it up behind the door. Don't know what's the matter with him, inviting people to lunch, like he had something in here to eat. It's these old-fashion habits of hospitality, the ones he learned as a child down in North Carolina, down on the homeplace. Up here in New York most folks long since forgotten how to act, don't know why he hadn't. Emmanuel stood over the sink, rubbed a little grime from the window, peering into the airshaft. *Uh-huh.* If Barry hadn't decided to get himself locked up, Emmanuel'd be up in Liberty, New York right now, looking at spring come in on his own property, nobody to bother him but his un-heartbroke wife and maybe a good dog. Little house, or a nice doublewide trailer on a cinderblock foundation he put in hisself. Little vegetable garden. Barry coulda stayed down here in the city, taking care of his own grandchild. Emmanuel decided to add an omelet to the soup he was planning to open. No reason for the boy to know them eggs was supposed to be breakfast for the rest of the week. He stirred eggs, decided he was just gonna have to find him a chess game. Maybe head down to Washington Square. Entertain a tourist or find him a college kid. From the front room he heard Akinde put on the radio, turn it down low. Tomato, or maybe chicken noodle? All kids like chicken noodle. Look like Campbell's putting some more meat in these cans. Emmanuel preferred some of these other soups, but you can't beat Campbell's prices. He could hear Akinde in front stealthily changing the stations, looking for something to listen to. News—talk—light music—R&B (he hesitated there a little while)—jazz (another hesitation)—news again—rock (pause)—rap (settled there). Emmanuel was disappointed. Have to show the boy some real music. Emmanuel had a decent collection, coupla CDs, but he preferred real records. He slid a perfect omelet onto a warm plate, congratulated himself. Cooking was something he missed, especially cooking for family and friends—the ones he still had. But all that cost money. So he gave up entertaining in favor of paying rent. Doctor didn't want him to eat anything but oatmeal anyway. Emmanuel dished out the soup, put a couple slices in the toaster. Whole wheat. Always liked brown bread. Emma Lee preferred the white. Her and Barry both.

Down home they always had the brown. His father wouldn't eat anything else. Meant his mama wouldn't make anything else. Barry started bringing his own bread in the house in high school, claimed the brown bread upset his stomach. Emmanuel laughed, remembering the old man's face. Never mind the gambling, till the day he died, Redman King was *convinced* Barry went wrong from eating that store-bought white bread. Emmanuel set out the soup, put out the toast and butter, brought out the omelet on one of Emma's good plates.

Akinde came in, washed his hands carefully, sat down and waited for grace. Something else Emmanuel taught him. Again

Emmanuel was struck by the boy's unnatural, unchildlike watchfulness. Akinde bent over his soup, eating with concentration, biding his time. He wanted something, Emmanuel could tell, watching the sharp little glances the boy sent up over his soupspoon. Emmanuel was put in mind of his hopeless nephew, Andre, this here boy's daddy. Andre always wanting something, every time you see him. Not much likeness to this boy, who favored his grandfather, but didn't have Barry's wild side. Still, Emmanuel had seen his brother looking just like that, holding his hand close and steady at yet another card table, yellow eyes successfully concealing any answers. Maybe he should go ahead, teach the boy chess, stifle his fear the boy would fall in love with games, gambling, the rambling random life, go the way his grandfather did, right out of life and down into unrecoverable darkness.

Emmanuel blessed the boy's African name—which wasn't Barry's, wasn't Andre's. Something new in the family, after all. Who would have thought Andre and that girl he found up at the Harlem River Houses would know how to name and thus grace a boychild. Who would have thought this child could be their child?

Well..., Emmanuel thought what he'd often thought, God must have him some sense of humor.

Akinde had finished his meal while Emmanuel was still working on his bowl of soup. Sat there politely waiting for him to finish, long feet restlessly tapping. Neither of them had much to say today, boy's long head must be as full of thoughts as his own. But they were easy together, comfortable—blood kin. Emmanuel slid his untouched half of the omelet onto Akinde's plate. Akinde just looked the question, and then ate it quickly with the same silent concentration. Emmanuel's heart ached a little. He can't be hungry? They got to feed him. *Nah*, he must just be looking for something made with a little attention. He'd have to show the boy how to cook a little. None of his people had ever been helpless in the kitchen—men or women. Emmanuel took out his pack of Gauloises—a bad habit he picked up in the Merchant Marines—and shook out the one cigarette a day he allowed himself. "Alright, Mister Akinde," he told the boy, "spill it." Boy looking at him all wide-eyed. Thought the old man was napping. Emmanuel grinned at him through the smoke, teeth a little yellowed in his oak dark face, but all of them his, *thank you, God.*

"I been talking to my caseworker," said Akinde, peeking up at him. Not a good beginning. If there was any word Emmanuel hated to hear, it was "caseworker." He wasn't raised up this way, didn't raise up his family to be this way.

"She said," continued Akinde, carefully, "you could get on the grandparent program, get a special stipend, extra help and stuff. She said, if you took both of us, me and Nikki, they might be able to get us into a bigger apartment."

Every word the boy uttered fell like a stone on Emmanuel's soul. Paperwork. Piles of forms. Endless visits to government office wastelands where he would sit on his butt for hours waiting for somebody to get around to him. God, hadn't he seen enough of that side of life when he was trying to save Barry—him and Emma both? Hadn't he? Take the pride of a working man, of a family man, into those offices and the first thing they do is try to crush it. Like when an ignorant man goes into church with a hat on. Folks be pouncing on him, "What are you doing with that up in *here?*" Akinde was watching him. Emmanuel couldn't tell if he'd put all his cards on the table or not. Emmanuel put his cigarette out.

"First place, you know I'm not your grandfather." All this was some more of Andre's mess. Some more of *Barry's* mess.

When Barry went to jail, Andre came to him, asked him to spend some time with the child—watchful, skinny little thing with his granddaddy's yellow eyes. Andre didn't tell him about the tissue of lies he constructed before he lit out for parts unknown.

"That don't matter," said Akinde, carefully. "They just call it the grandparent program. It's for any family. Any family member that wants to take a child."

"Second place," continued Emmanuel, "I am an old man. A tired man." Akinde's face slowly stilled, froze, narrowed, and drew to a point around his tightly drawn mouth. The lids of his eyes slid down until the golden light in them was shuttered. Emmanuel turned his own eyes away.

"Too old and too tired to fill out applications, have a bunch of strangers calling me by my first name and come peek in my bedroom drawers. Treat me the way I wouldn't treat an animal in the zoo."

"That's alright, Uncle Manny," Akinde told him from behind this new narrow face. Emmanuel didn't like it. 'Course the boy was mad, he only called him "uncle" when he wanted to make a point. But that was what he was, this boy's great-uncle, never mind his slickster nephew Andre and his crazy scheme to replace his father. Akinde stood up, ready to take his too-formal leave. "Thank you for lunch," he said with his careful, unchildlike courtesy. Boy put a little white business card on the coffee table without comment. Emmanuel could read upside down: *Administration for Children's Services.* Then Akinde left, gave him one backward glance, enigmatic, pinched, but he still had a bit of that other look too: Barry with a hole card.

When he was gone, Emmanuel took revenge on the dishes, scrubbing the two pots mercilessly. Even got out the copper cleaner. Think that same jar been under the sink since Emma Lee died. Emmanuel put water in the dried-up paste, stood over

126

the sink brooding. The whole thing was entirely the fault of Andre MacKaskel King—idiot, fool, con man—and *he* was entirely the fault of Barry Redman King—wastrel, gambler, prodigal. Yeah, them and the assorted women they took up with and put down. Boy was really a grass orphan, him and his baby sister both.

The familiar smell that rose up out of the little jar of green paste made his nose run and his eyes water. Emma'd used it on her pots every night. He wasn't any slouch in the kitchen, but he didn't keep house to her standards. When this was her kitchen, them pots hung out on the wall gleaming like jewelry. And what happened to Emma Lee's yellow lace curtains used to screen the airshaft from view? Emmanuel wondered fruitlessly where they had gone... Yellow lace birds picked out of yellow lace fabric, alive in the wind. In the course of Jerome's brief and hopeful life, those lacy birds were one thing he loved. Little fat baby hands waving, while Emma laughed and fussed and tried to feed him. Just more lost and missing things... Run him out of his apartment where the further corners of the closets still held her scent and every surface had been touched—been blessed— by her. All so Barry—Andre—Akinde could break his heart all over again. They already got all his money, now they come back for his pride, like burglars left something behind too heavy to carry away first time they broke in.

After lunch, Emmanuel was restless, couldn't settle. So he went downstairs, found his friend Wild Willie G. and tried to explain himself. Wild Willie setting up the chessboard while he talked, hoping to win one on the sly while Emmanuel was distracted. Willie's three-legged dog slinking around wall-eyed. Emmanuel did find that dog distracting, with his lopsided gait, and sorta crazy look—another gambler alright. Wild Bill knew all that, might be why he kept that dog around, dog won more games than Bill Tilly ever did, William like to keep folks off-balance and distracted, like a circus act or a good magician—or a man with a whole lotta names. Emmanuel told him the story, which Willie already knew, but had the courtesy to hear out in silence, which Emmanuel appreciated. Maybe he should let Willie win a game.

"Way I see it," said Wild Bill, and slid a piece forward in sly invitation, "they should be women around for that kinda thing. What about that other grandma? Boy don't have him no aunties?" Emmanuel moved a knight automatically. *Uh oh*, now he was playing and couldn't quit without a forfeit.

Emmanuel grumbled back, "Emma used to say, whenever they come across anythin' they don't want to do, men volunteer them some women."

Wild Willie grinned at him, "Salty tongue on her, yo' wife." Yeah, right, just happy 'cause he got his game.

"Anyway," Willie went on, "you got the boy a job down at Mac's. You takin' care of him." Willie stroked the edge of his inlaid chessboard. He wouldn't play on the park tables.

Emmanuel shook his head, distracted. Willie's easy sanction fell on him like a whip.

"Never play distracted," that was one of Barry's maxims. Emmanuel didn't hold with gambling—which is what he was doing right now, five dollars rode on every game with Willie—but back in the day, he did love to sit back and watch his brother play. Barry was alive at the poker table, concentrating, yellow eyes shining, fingers full of magic, gambling his last dime away or winning a week of a working man's wages. *Yeah, a man shouldn't sit down at the table unless he can put his mind to it,* Emmanuel reminded himself fiercely, trying to shake himself to attention, but his mind kept wandering. That thoughtless opening put him in a weak position. And that cream-colored dog of

Willie's limped back and forth across his field of vision, inviting him to wonder just how it stayed upright…. Emmanuel jerked himself back to the game with an effort. 'Cause, let's face it, he couldn't afford to lose them five dollars.

The regulars gathered to enjoy a battle of the giants. It was an overcast afternoon, with spring temporarily in retreat, the quiet lull before the kids got out of school. The regulars not talking much, just standing around taking instruction. Despite the disquiet that lay across his mind, Emmanuel began to enjoy the match. Wild Bill got busy losing in a style that Emmanuel hadn't seen from him before, flinging the wrong pieces into sacrificial positions, one or two moves after it would have done him some good. The pattern of the game's future rose clear in Emmanuel's mind—like the pattern dancers would make if you could float like a dreamer above a ballroom floor. This was the beauty of chess. He'd tried to teach it to his family, failed with all of them. Barry said the game was slow, but Emmanuel believed that his brother couldn't love a game without an element of chaos and chance. Andre—bless him—didn't have the brains. Emma Lee resented the rules—acted like he made them up to fret her. His boy Jerome was too little, Emmanuel had just started to teach him checkers when he got sick.

Maybe he should try again with Akinde. Boy had the concentration—*bad move, Willie*—had the brains, had the gravity. But no, after this, he would quit coming around, forget about his "granddaddy." Emmanuel would just be ole Uncle Manny up in Harlem. "Funny, when I was little, I used to think he was my grandfather." No reason in the world why Emmanuel should find himself choking on a taste like dust and ashes. No reason. 'Cept maybe…somewhere, somethin' precious might be dying.

Willie's wall-eyed partner was watching him with an ear cocked and a distinct expression of disappointment. Emmanuel looked up, found Willie waiting on him. His own legendary patience deserted him and he made a move blindly, then, too late, he saw an alteration ahead in the pattern. He just had to hope Wild Willie didn't notice it.

After the game Mister Till was expansive, enlarged. Offering round warm cans of no-name soda like it was the refreshment of kings. Not that he wasn't used to winning, just not used to beating Mister Emmanuel King. Emmanuel took a can to sooth his throat. He was amused by Willie's inability to let the game remain a game, a liability he could always exploit later. Cream-colored dog circled the two of them in lopsided triumph, grinning his wall-eyed grin at the loser. Willie offered him another game, but Emmanuel declined. This wasn't helping. He paid Willie his money, then watched his old friend instruct a youngster for a while. Didn't want to go home, thought about going back up to the zoo, visit with the wolf again, but another eight dollars on top of the five he just lost to Willy? Plus all them eggs he fed the boy for lunch? At this rate he was never gonna make it till Monday, when his Social Security kicked in. He decided to head on over to the local branch library, Countee Cullen, a bit of a walk, but worth it, if it helped settle his mind.

On the way over there, all he could see was the boy's face, see it running through the changes, traveling that short distance between sad and sorry. See that new narrow-face look. And he wasn't satisfied with circumstances, wasn't satisfied with himself, wasn't satisfied at all.

In the library, Emmanuel took a seat at the long table down by the quiet end, near the history section, science and natural history around the corner. Had a couple of books about wolves to look at while watching people come and go, Emmanuel thinking long and hard between turning the pages. Nobody stayed, which suited him. Sometimes he felt sociable, help out a child doing homework or somebody struggling with English or some paperwork, but not today. African man sat down, read a tissue-thin letter, read it again, folded it up thoughtfully, tucked it up in an envelope and took it away. Emmanuel coveted the stamps, couldn't remember why, then—*wave*—it was Jerome had the passion for far-away places. Lord. Emma didn't like him encouraging it with maps, foreign stamps, old copies of *National Geographic*, model sailboats. She saw her baby growing up, getting away, maybe another sailor boy in the family, which was Emmanuel's not-so-secret dream. Sadly, they both ended up disappointed, but the boy got away. Yes, he got away. Emmanuel supposed Akinde was too old to start collecting stamps. Hard to keep up with what they wanted, what they needed, what was suitable. Yesterday it was an action figure or a picture book, today it was a house to live in and the last few years of a man's life.

He had the table to himself a little while, then here come a chunky boy. Boy sat hisself down hard, shaking the table, started working on a paper. Scribble, peek, scribble, peek, pause to bite at his pencil, squinty-eyed boy with one of them square heads. Maybe two inches of hard-bitten pencil left. Boy writing heavy-handed on the front and back of every single sheet of paper. Barry used to say, "Never sit down to the table with a square head man, you lose *all* your money."

Emmanuel's back gave a warning twinge as he bent back over one of his books. An empty armchair with a sagging seat invited him from across the room, but, *uh uh, no*, fall asleep up in here, be all embarrassed when the little librarian, Ms. McKenna, came creeping around, have to wake him up so she could go on home. Sat up in the straightback chair, still turning the pages of the book, soothed by the beauty of some of the photographs, reading a word here or there, and then reading on with more attention.

Square head boy finished the attack on his paper, shot Emmanuel a hot look of contempt and flung hisself out the room. From his seat Emmanuel could lift his head, see that boy go striding down 136th street, head down like a bull or a bison. Emmanuel grinned to himself. There was a boy was never gonna win any popularity contests.

He turned another page, and, *hello*, here come a wolf, could be his gray brother up at the zoo, wolf giving him a yellow-eyed look from page seventy-six of the library book. Emmanuel spent couple minutes with the picture, wishing he had a copy, looking deep into the dark bordered eyes of the wolf, drooping lower over the pages. He fell into a reverie and from there into a dream, drifting off in a remembered smell of Elmer's Glue and tempera paint, his boy Jerome's high laugh ringing some-where—but always behind him. And then the gray brother came walking over the pages of his book and into his dream... with a question.

Restin', just restin', Emmanuel replied, shifting his weight on his dream thighs. Wolf told him he was *old*.

And gettin' older, Emmanuel told him. *Easy*, said the wolf, *for an elder to lose his way. You have a young one to guide you?*

That made Emmanuel laugh out loud. Laugh had an echoey quality in the spaces of the dream. *'Mong our folks, it's the old ones 'pposed to do the leadin', young ones 'pposed to follow—not that they always do.*

Backwards, grunted the wolf. He tilted his head and looked at Emmanuel out of wise yellow, wolfish eyes. *Take my advice, avoid the foolishness of the tall people and find a young one to guide you. One*, the dreamwalker told him, *whose dreams are still fresh.* The wolf tilted his head the other way. In the dreaming distance,

Emmanuel heard a chorus of wolfish howls. He listened in the dream, wondering, told the wolf, *funny I didn't know it was music.*

Gray brother grinned, *You hear the chorus. Wolves,* said the wolf, *wolves are walking the world.*

Nah, said Emmanuel. *That's all gone. All the wide territory, all the wild places. I used to roam the sea. Now I live in a box.*

No, instructed the wolf as he turned away, *You live on an island. The island lives in a sea. The island lives in time. And time is wide.*

Emmanuel woke with a start, already ashamed of himself—sleeping in public! But his corner was deserted and the librarians unnoticing, barricaded behind their little fortress of desks and paper. Emmanuel laughed a little—like somebody gonna break in here and steal all the books.

There was a hush around him, a long brown silence put Emmanuel in mind of the libraries of his childhood. The only sound was children's laughter down the basement, some kind of story hour or craft project in progress. Memory gave him a pinch. Longtime ago now, he used to bring Jerome and then Andre by here on Saturdays, supposed to be giving him and Emma Lee a break, but half the time ended up staying hisself, caught up in popsicle sticks, Elmer's Glue and Dr. Seuss.

He took the photography book back over to Ms. McKenna, busy trying to close up, but she gave him a sweet smile when she returned his driver's license. Emmanuel emerged into a cool, clear twilight hush. Lucky... found him the few magical instants perfectly balanced between day and night. Paused on the steps, breathing deeply and missing people and bygone things: Emma Lee's sharp tongue and her sweetly observant eye, Barry's crazy go-to-hell grin, first deep roll of a good ship leaving port, the wicked belly laughter of sailors, Jerome's sticky little hands, and *oh yeah,* the way people used to be, and *uh-huh,* the way tomatoes used to taste.

Tuesday morning Emmanuel woke up, still uneasy in his mind and now feeling it little in his stomach. Couldn't remember why, thought it might be the usual Tuesday blues—waking up and knowing he'd saved up all that aggravation for one day. Social Security, electric, gas, phone, dental visits, his jail ministry, hospital, nursing home, landlord/tenant court, free clinic, cemetery, IRS, *oh Lord,* long list of things a body would just as soon skip. Emmanuel rolled, shifted his weight over to his good hip, his eye landing on Emma's picture at the back of the night table behind his reading glasses. He groaned.

Oh, yeah, the boy. Always was Emma's pet—him and his daddy both. Emmanuel sat up, remembering Akinde's visit yesterday and the full weight of everything fell on him again.

Dragging himself out of bed, unrefreshed, he started the day sipping a suitably bitter cup of coffee and munching a couple slices of dry brown bread toast. Doctor be pleased, next thing to bread and water.

On the kitchen table, he'd laid out today's paperwork and he spent his breakfast perversely staring at it. Social Security card, lost and stolen check replacement forms, *uh-huh,* third time now. 'Lectric. Cut-off notice. Bad, but not as bad as it could be. Lights still on, no payment agreement broken. Wiping his mouth with a piece of paper towel, Emmanuel got up on the step stool and got fifty dollars out of his emergency stash, money he usually pretended wasn't there. Just being hungry didn't count as an emergency. Keeping the lights on did. He used Emma Lee's old flour canister as a bank, kept his flour, sugar and coffee in the refrigerator, which she never would. She liked to see those yellow cans lined up with names in red spelling out the ingredients. Sometimes she'd shake things up, keep sugar in the "tea" canister, tea in the "coffee" canister. One time Emmanuel went to get flour for his gumbo, found the corn meal box and the cornstarch box snuggled up next to each in the "flour" can, no sign of the flour, meanwhile his *roux* is sticking to the pan. Emmanuel smiled, thinking about Emma Lee and her ways, wishing he could remember what he did with her yellow lace curtains—he could hang them curtains back up in the window, see them birds again shaking in the breeze. He sat smiling, sipping coffee, but then feeling better for some reason, got up and put some cream in his cup.

Peeking out from under the 'lectic bill envelope (red-bordered so your neighbors know all your business) was the card Akinde left him yesterday with his social worker's name on it. Emmanuel asked himself if he was going to talk to the woman or what?

Day was ruined whether he went up there or not. At his age, Emmanuel was jealous of his days. Supposed she called him, talking about he had to come down there—on a Monday? Or a Thursday, when Emmanuel liked to spend his time near salt water—on a boardwalk, down in the port, out on the Brooklyn Bridge—anywhere he could see the sea.

Plus there was that note from the clinic, so it was either the doctor or the social worker. Doctor wouldn't call and he had a month or two on the yellow pills. Besides, he thought hopefully, Akinde just a boy. What does he know about programs and paperwork? One look at him, social worker be making excuses up for him. He got up without thinking, buttered half a poppy seed bagel, a fresh one from the top of the bag. What kinda social worker put a teenage boy and a baby girl in with an old man by hisself in a little apartment with no money? Where them kids 'pposed to sleep? Bring along that cut-off notice, hold it so she can see it. Emmanuel finished his breakfast with another cup of coffee and cream, well, half and half. They don't have real cream anymore up in the city.

Putting on his gray suit with a white dress shirt and silver tie, Emmanuel gave himself a grin in the mirror, didn't think he looked too bad. Everything a little out-of-date, but nobody expect an old man to be up-to-date, folks get a little suspicious if you look too good. Maybe he could get through the day without some thirty-year-old stranger calling him "Emmanuel." Should get him a name tag, like his boy Jerome used to wear on class trips, pin it to the front of his gray suit, little tag say "Mister King."

Emmanuel added a hat and his walking stick and went down to the park in his dress clothes. Willie had got hisself a game going. A few of the regulars watching intently, plus the before (and during) school crowd. Emmanuel intended to go on by with a greeting, but wait a minute… He chuckled, Wild Willie had hisself a tiger by the tail this time. Square head boy with book bag between his legs saying "Stuyvesant High School." Had some books in that bag. Had him some moves, some textbook-new and shiny moves, but—*lookit that*—the boy's gone and added some wicked little twists, surprising Willie, surprising Emmanuel, who settled down to enjoy the match, forgetful of his time. Boy sipping plain water in a no-label bottle, gnawing on a thumbnail. Willie G. looking rueful, even that three-legged partner of his looking all put out. And ain't that the same square head boy from the library yesterday? Cain't be a wave, must be that same boy, look at him, played chess just like he wrote them papers, nibble, sip, peek, *check*, nibble, sip, peek. *checkmate.*

William G. Tilly wasn't a good loser. Made him sour and evil, but let's be fair, thought Emmanuel, he didn't have a lot of practice losing. Barry always told him, "Losing teach you more than winning."

Square head boy stood up, all business, collected and counted up his money like a store clerk, all five bills, snap, snap, snap, packed up his water and schoolbag, gave Willie a tight little nod; disappeared in the direction of the train before the observers could get his name. They clucked and cackled over that, disapproving, liking to pick over a good game with both parties. Emmanuel laughing, here that boy beat Willie and not even late to class. He edged closer to his friend, leaned over the board, surveyed the damage, cleared his throat, "Barry always told me you never—"

"—sit down to the table with a square-headed man," interrupted his friend, the evil Mister Till. Willie stuck a toothpick between his full brown lips, started chewing, squinting into the sun, brand new straw dress hat set flat on his big head. "What am I supposed to do? Tell that boy he cain't have a game 'cause he got him a square head?"

Emmanuel just grinned at him. Willie frowned into the sun, sat there trying to give Emmanuel the evil eye, but then found himself grinning back. Dog grinning too, flopping happily at Wild Bill's big feet, temporarily off the clock. Dog taking hisself a well-earned break, animal worked harder than half the folks Emmanuel knew, should put him in a chess book with his own damn page of wins and losses.

Emmanuel and Willie sat there, enjoying each other's company. Boys out in the back having that old, old argument they like to have 'bout three-dimensional chess. Emmanuel grunted, *3-D chess, humph.*

Willie laughed, "Them boys have enough trouble with regular old flat chess which is, as you know, dimensional enough if you know how to play." He started counting off on his big fingers, "Les' see, you got time..."

"...space," agreed Emmanuel.

"...will...mind," continued Willie.

"Not sure you can call them dimensions," said Emanuel.

"When you talkin' 'bout chess they are," said Willie. "Rest of life too…emotion…"

"And motion."

"…and somethin' else." Wild Willie concluded for both of them, with a fat snap of his big fingers.

Oh yeah…that indefinable—something else. Talked about it with Barry once. Looking at him through the foggy plexiglas, smelling the bad smells all around, hearing the broken-up families, looking into Barry's yellow eyes—very clear they were, those eyes, the last time he saw his brother. Back in North Carolina, they always called them kinda light eyes, yellow dog eyes. But Barry's eyes put Emmanuel in mind of some other kinda animal. Something wild.

Funny thing though, locked up, Barry rediscovered the touch, rediscovered the love of the game. *Yeah,* Emmanuel was desperate, but his brother's eyes were clear and even serene, as they rested on him, through the plexiglas, the last time they talked.

"Player takes every factor in the game, adds himself. What's the result of that sum? When the player is added to the game?" Barry just calm and instructive as a professor in a classroom. Emmanuel felt like tellin' him, "You in *here!* You *locked up!*" But those yellow eyes didn't care, well, anymore than they ever did. As his brother instructed him, those eyes watched Emmanuel— as remote, as untouchable, as mysterious as the eyes of any free thing.

"Where you going all dressed up?" Willie broke into his thoughts. "Here it is Tuesday, so must be somethin' you don't wanna do." Emmanuel handed him the social worker's card. Willie looked at it in silence, put it down on the edge of the board. "This about Akinde and his sister." Not a question.

Emmanuel felt a flare of irritation. Willie, as usual, all *up* in his business. But the irritation subsided as quickly as it came. Willie giving him a look, grinning with all his teeth…*who you tryin' to kid, Manny?* Yeah, Willie know everything. Emmanuel nodded.

Willie opened a can of his no-name cola. Took a long sip. Offered one to Emmanuel, who refused, even though this early in the day, 'least that cola was cold. Emmanuel sitting there trying to figure out how long *had* he known Willie? When'd he meet him? When he first showed up in New York? Just another second cousin with a third hand suitcase and a dog-eared note from somebody's grandma… Or was it all the way back to North Carolina? Was Willie that little boy used to sit outside Miz Kritchen's with a rag ball and a stick looking for a game? Emmanuel couldn't be sure, shook his head. He was only too familiar with the treacherous, slippery quality of memory.

"You gonna do it?" asked Willie G.

"No, I am not," said Emmanuel. "I am too old and too tired to take on them youngins. Aside from which, the fact is that I do not have any money."

"Then why you goin' down there?" asked Wild Bill.

"Somebody from the family got to go, see about they interests," said Emmanuel.

"You gonna do it." Willie took a sip of his no-name cola.

"I am not. Let me remind you that I am not those children's grandfather."

"Now mind you, I'm not saying you *should* do it." Willie G. leaned back, took a handkerchief from his pocket, wiped cool moisture from the can, stroked his face, the back of his neck and his throat. "But you that boy's grandfather. 'Least the only one he ever knew. You let him believe it, all the time he was growing up. Way I see it, you owe him what you'd owe your own grandchild, whatever that would be. I couldn't do it, *nah, uh uh*, but we talkin' what you would do. And you know, Emmanuel, I know you, and you are not gonna be able to leave them kids out there. Nikki be alright, cute lil' baby girl like that. But who in the world gonna want that big ole boy?"

Electric wasn't too bad. Emmanuel went there first to avoid the before-work crush at the Social Security. Man behind the desk was polite, addressing him as "Mr. King," and filling out the payment agreement with an admirable neutrality of tone Emmanuel appreciated. He was out on the street before he had to resort to his book. Emmanuel always brought a book as insurance against boredom on Tuesdays, although usually the knot in his stomach prevented him from reading with any real attention. Carrying a chess book today, playing games in his head helped with the tension, the weight of the book in his pocket pulling his jacket out of line, a habit Emma Lee had hated, especially when he brought a book into church, trying to pretend like it was a Bible.

Emmanuel shook his head, today, he had to stay focused on the here-and-now, not drift off into the past. He walked the few blocks to the Social Security.

Guard made him empty his pockets, then tried to twist his cane apart. Emmanuel kept setting off the metal detector. Finally a girl come back with an electric wand, ran it over him, people stopping to look and Emmanuel embarrassed and feeling like a criminal. Which is why he preferred to stay out of these places. They gave him back his belongings in a plastic box. Emmanuel rode the elevator up in a bemused and thoughtful state.

The wait at Social Security was gonna be longer, which he had expected. He took a seat on a smooth wooden bench near the windows, better than one of them little plastic bucket chairs. Some of them cracked, pinch your behind if you're not careful. Wished he could smoke. Worse thing about visiting places like this, you leave knowing half dozen stories sadder than your own. You could hear folks in the offices, at the counters, pleading, excusing, begging.

Plus, people liked to talk to Emmanuel while they waited, bring him they little bits of paper, looking for advice and explanations. Here come a little Spanish woman looking all lost, grandchild tucked under her arm, spotted Emmanuel and hustled over to grab the seat next to him, all cozy and confiding like she'd known him for years. Emmanuel's Spanish was pretty good, something else he picked up in the Merchant Marine. "*Hóla, Senora,*" he said. Woman's face brightened up and they picked through her little cache of documents together, trying to figure out what she was supposed to have. She had family photographs stuck in at random among the paperwork, one in particular struck Emmanuel, little gap-tooth girl in ribbons and braids, must be this same lady sitting here beside him looking for a death benefit on her father, made it to ninety-seven, well good for him. Emmanuel took another look at the peeking grandchild, *uh-huh,* same face, not his wave, but here it is anyway.

Lady had a pretty face, nut-brown, round, tired. She was a foot shorter than him, had to peer up at his face. Kept telling him, "*Gracias. Gracias, senor.*"

"*Por nada,*" he told her. She was wearing a sweat suit, brightly colored, printed all over with a wicked looking fairy tale wolf running and hiding and peeking out at a merry gingerbread boy. Like something she borrowed from a grandchild, one a little bigger than the girl under her arm. While Emmanuel went through her papers, finally locating what she needed, his eye kept wandering back to her jacket. Look at Story Wolf winking at him from her sleeve. Story Wolf talking about how he won, how he lost, about his disguises and his tricks, about his mysteries. Story Wolf telling him to go *under* if he couldn't go over, go *'round* if he couldn't go through.

Emmanuel found himself on the street around lunchtime, tired and dispirited. No air in these government offices and not much daylight either. Hard on a man like him—a man who spent his whole working life around ships, on or near the water. At sea, he could go out on deck, see for miles in every direction. No limits to a man's vision. Something Emma Lee didn't understand, only time she came on board. All she saw were narrow bunks, cramped spaces, the tight mess, the little heads where you had to be flexible to do your business. That was his last ship, the Liberty Ship *Paul Laurence Dunbar*—proud name for a fine ship.

Even when he'd left the sea, left the hard roll for the flat land, he was still down to the port every day, down where land meets water, making iron and steel and wood into ships and setting them out on the water. Hearing and smelling the sea every day, feeling that satisfaction. First up in Brooklyn at the Navy Yard, then out in Hoboken, New Jersey, thirty years at the Todd Shipworks. Emma Lee wanted him closer, tried to get him to take the postal exam. She had a cousin in the Manhattanville Station Branch, but Emmanuel put his foot down. Some things you cain't do even for a woman like Emma.

Emmanuel sighed, drained. Too many memories. He took himself over to McDonald's and spent one of his lonely looking dollars on a salad.

He remembered to tuck extra napkins in his pocket at the service island. Sat over his salad, picking at it without appetite. He could just skip the rest of bad ole Tuesday and head on back. Emmanuel sighed again, *Tuesdays*. Well, tomorrow he'd rest up, stay close to home. Thursday, he'd be near the water.

He pushed the salad away, gave up fighting the knot in his

stomach. Put it in the trash, a waste, but it couldn't be helped, he wasn't going down to the Children's Services with a doggy bag. He took a few more napkins to compensate, then walked over to the office, just a couple of blocks. Van went by full of colored men, taking prisoners to court, sad faces at the windows. Which is how Emmanuel felt going into the building. Mostly women walking in all heavy-footed. The ones coming out, moving with a little more bounce. Emmanuel envied them.

He hesitated in the lobby, aware the guards were looking at him, maybe laughing at an old man, don't know where he supposed to be. Didn't help he was the only man in here, 'cept for the guards. *Okay, les' do this, if we're gonna do it,* he told himself.

Submitting to another search, now Emmanuel was remembering Barry, time he stole that pack of cards out at Miz Kritchen's candy store. Might have been his first pack of cards. Kept them out in the back, in the shed, 'cause you *know* Daddy didn't 'low no cards in the house. Emmanuel was with him, eight years old, just a pup. Emmanuel remembering how startled he was when his brother slipped the pack in a pocket, same time winking at him, and pushing him out the store. Had to push hard 'cause Emmanuel's legs had stopped working. Barry's hot breath in his ear, "Go!" That was the first bitter discovery: that his well-loved brother couldn't be trusted, that his brother would take him into dark places, all the time smiling. Emmanuel, an old man, still haunted by his brother's yellow-eyed wink. Remembered swinging his head back, catching a glimpse of Miz Kritchen's face through the greasy glass, *oh yeah,* she knew. But didn't tell. That was Barry. Benefiting, as usual, from the love everybody had for him.

Guard waving him through, impatient, here he is holding up the line again. Emmanuel followed the heavy-footed women into the offices, gave the social worker's card to the girl at the desk. She slapped a form on the counter. *Uh, huh, yeah, here we go.* Chained-up pen ran dry while he was trying to write out the boy's name. Chain too short for a lefthander. Emmanuel couldn't speak. Could barely nod. His mouth was stopped with ashes, tasting of the unforgiven past.

Emmanuel expected—wanted—to sit for a while, settle himself, but—wouldn't you know it—here come the girl to take him right back. Down a dark hallway. Round a couple twisty corners. Pinchfaced woman came out to meet them and Emmanuel's heart dropped, but here it turnt out she was only another guide. Place so big they had to have two, Emmanuel snorted. More corners, down narrow aisles, place full of misery. Pass a little boy sitting by himself on a table, pants stained, crying, uncomforted, broken toy under the table. Turnt another corner, here another old man with his head down on a desk. Now you got a whole family sleeping in chairs. Down another hall. Guide took him to a cubicle: "Ms. Jewelle Church" on the wall next to the door. His guide offered him her pinchfaced smile, left him there.

Busy woman, Ms. Jewelle Church, on the phone, on the computer, also trying to eat some lunch, pencils stuck all in her hair. She waved him to a seat. Emmanuel watching her try and do all that, studying her, couldn't help liking what he saw. Honest looking face, little sweaty now, but warm in here, no windows, no air, little fan clacking away in the corner, not helping much. Still Emmanuel thought she looked kind, sensible, not like the kind of woman who'd put a teenager and a baby girl in with an old man with no money. Emmanuel shuffled papers in his lap, made sure the electric cut-off was on top, big red type, see it across the room: "Open Immediately." Far cry from the days when he and Emma paid all their bills on time and put something in the bank.

Ms. Church mouthed something at him, probably "be right with you." Emmanuel smiled at her, went on studying the office, trying to get a feel for the person spent her days there. Broken drawer on the file cabinet duct-taped shut, brick up under the credenza, *uh-oh*, here's a woman little too used to making do. Over her shoulder, a bulletin board, cards, photos, notices stuck up and a calendar from the Sierra Club, "Save our Wilderness." Fan jerked around and blew, May page—wild ducks—flew up, he could see June. Fan turnt back, June was hidden. Another gust of hot air. June revealed. June was a wolf, seen close-up, greeny-grey-yellow eyes gleaming. While Ms. Church fussed and fretted on her call, Emmanuel studied the hidden then revealed face of the wolf.

June Wolf was lighter—had a cream-colored ruff—than his wolf in the zoo. June Wolf was a mother, bit of a cub's black muzzle showing below her face, licking. Here's June Wolf looking at him, asking him what he was going to do.

Emmanuel told her they wasn't his children.

Emmanuel told her he toiled in harness long enough and this was his time to run free.

I carried the weight, he told her, *carried it far*.

Carry it further, she demanded.

This here Andre's burden, his weight, Emmanuel told her. *His children*.

And where is he? she answered. *You know he's among the lost. The lost carry no burdens. We run on without them.*

Barry, he whispered.

Your brother? You are too wise not to forgive the fallen. Too wise to wait on the lost. The pack is diminished. But you remain.

June Wolf's face rippled on the page, the cub nuzzling her. Emmanuel sat waiting for a stranger to tell what was gonna happen to his brother's grandchildren.

Ms. Church got herself off the phone, smiling, talking, pulling out paperwork, forms, files, turning to her computer and side-sneaking a bite of lunch. In the foreground, Emmanuel was listening, her words dropping like stones on to his heart: home visits, supervision, custody, housing allowance, income assistance, doctor's certificate, physiological evaluation, criminal background check. Seem like the woman was pulling out a form for every word. In the background, Emmanuel was still talking to June Wolf. He asked June Wolf—*God help him*—was he really gonna try and do this crazy thing?

And June Wolf told him that he was.

In the foreground he went back to paying attention to Ms. Church. Here she is asking him if he had the fingerprint form she gave Akinde to give him. Talking about it's only $75 and he'd get reimbursed from the grandparent program in, *oh*, no more than three months.

"No, Ma'am," said Emmanuel. "Guess the boy forgot." He smiled at her. *Uh-huh*, Akinde knew better than to put something like that in front of him. She kept on holding that pink fingerprint form out like it was an invitation to a party he wouldn't want to miss on any account. Emmanuel lied easily, "Oh, no, Ma'am. Don't need that. My prints on file with the gover'ment, Merchant Marine, World War II."

Like Story Wolf tolt him, go 'round.

Form wavered in the air a minute, then she took it back, reluctantly, slid it back in the file where Emmanuel held out hope it'd get lost. She smiled a little and he smiled back, good-hearted woman with too many papers piled up in front of her, not enough sunlight.

Ms. Church whipped herself out another form, "I'll just take down some basic information." Emmanuel groaned—to himself, he thought—but she looked up, startled, so he must have done it out loud.

"Age?" she asked crisply, started filling in blanks rapidly with her stubby, hard-bitten pencil. Emmanuel could see she was one champion form-filler-inner.

"Seventy-eight." Ms. Church shook her head at him like he could do something about that.

"Full name? Social Security number? Last employment? Military service?" Rapid fire. Well, 'least she wasn't into wasting his time.

"Income?" she inquired, delicately.

Emmanuel told her, "Social Security." *Yeah,* that really made her shake her head.

"Property?"

Emmanuel shook his head, "Sold off."

Black eyes on him, judging him. She put the form down. "Mr. King, I have to tell you, some of what you're telling me doesn't make sense. Unless you're concealing facts." She took a sip from her coffee cup, eyes steady on him above the rim, little crescent bitten out of the styrofoam hinting at how she spent her days. Emmanuel let the silence hang, finally told her, "I had some setbacks."

"What do you mean by that, Mr. King?"

"Problems, family problems. Medical, legal problems."

"How does that impact on, say," she glanced down at her form, "Your lack of a pension after 15 years at Brooklyn Marine and another 20 years at Todd Shipyard? With that income you wouldn't necessarily qualify for additional assistance."

"My brother Barry got hisself in some trouble down in Atlantic City. These children's granddaddy. Always was a gambler. Never had a job. But he was good at it. Always made money. Spent ever' penny he made, too. Spent a lot on the family. When my boy was sick, he helped. Helped a lot. Leukemia.

They couldn't do much then, but Barry, he never would give up hope. Me and my wife, we spent ever' thing we had. When the insurance refused to pay, Barry was there, with his gambling money. Then, when it came time, he paid for the funeral too." Emmanuel paused for breath. Ms. Church got up, left her cubicle and brought him back a little trembly paper cup full of water. She handed it to him silently and he drank it down gratefully. Considerate.

"Later on, he lost the touch. Couldn't accept it. Kept on gambling. Kept on losing too. I told him what he always told me, 'Walk away.' He couldn't do it. Wanted it back. It was all he knew. All he had—way he lived. Then he run out of money to play. Borrowed from the wrong folks, made the wrong kind of deals, got involved in some things he shouldn't have. Ended up in jail. No, no, don't put that down in them children's papers." Ms. Church stopped writing. Emmanuel sighed. She was just gonna write it down the minute he left anyway. Well, at least he wouldn't have to watch. Something Emma Lee never understood, how the stain of the thing would touch ever'body in the family, how none'a them would escape. Here it is again, reaching out to touch another generation.

"What was your brother arrested for?"

"Lawyer called it self-defense," Emmanuel told her. "Might have been'a little premature," he conceded. That old, old habit: defending Barry, excusing Barry. Why? Barry was past excuse, gone beyond defense. What was she gonna put down when he left? Probably "criminal family background" and "violent tendencies." Well, she could look up the details for herself on the computer, no need to drag it out of him. How Barry ran out of options in that city of last resort, disgraced his folks and broke his brother's heart, left him to play daddy and granddaddy and mourn his reckless narrow behind in the long years stretching out ahead. He stretched out his fingers, feeling the stiffness. Noticed the electric bill still in his lap and shuffled it under the pile. Trying to remember, trying to be fair to the memories. "We wanted to help. Me and my wife spent what we had. Wasn't enough. Still had a lot of medical bills after Jerome died. Plus I had to take care of my daddy. Sold some property, got Barry another lawyer. First one they got him was no good. Ran out of money to pay the lawyer and Barry's trial coming up. Didn't have nothing else left, so I signed the pensions over to the lawyer to get him to represent Barry at the trial."

"Oh, Mr. King," said Ms. Church. "Was that wise? Or even legal?"

Emmanuel grimaced. Emma Lee might be gone, but a man could always find some woman to tell him, "I told you so." Even if she hadn't. "Lawyer wrote it up."

"Both pensions were reassigned? For how long?"

"For life. And he's younger than me."

Ms. Church shook her head. Her fingers twitched, maybe wanting to write "lack of judgment" along side of "no income." She looked at him with frank curiosity, probably dying to ask him if his wife went along with this crazy scheme. Emmanuel watched her shake off further questions, get briskly back to the business at hand, pulling out yet another form.

Meanwhile, from behind her curtain of May, June Wolf whispered, *A pisstail thing. To run on before your mate.*

"I need written confirmation of this . . . transfer from the assignee." Ms. Church made a note. "What happened to your brother?"

"Died in prison 'fore we could go to trial. Lawyer said Barry coulda won. Anyway, he had the agreement."

"Oh." Ms. Church averted her eyes, the way nice people do from a car wreck, started to write, then remembered she wasn't supposed to be taking that part down. She folded her hands, sat looking at the form for a minute with her mouth a little pursed. Emmanuel admired her restraint. Not too many women who could stop with just one "I told you so." Little fan yanked itself back with a whine, blew another gust, here she is again, June Wolf with her whispers, her yellowy-greeny eyes, seems like there's been a wolf looking in on him wherever he goes—like visitations from the wild.

"Now, Mr. King, let me see if I'm clear on all the circumstances. Both parents are...missing. Grandparents on both sides dead. No aunts or uncles. Ordinarily a granduncle, especially— excuse me—one in your age bracket wouldn't be the best candidate for kinship fostering. But I will tell you frankly, I haven't been able to place Akinde in the best situation. He's in one of our group homes. A lot of children do well there and I've urged Akinde to try to make the adjustment." She fiddled with the folder, "It's not a perfect situation, but realistically, it's the best we can do for him right now."

Emmanuel shifted his feet, adjusted his face to a careful blankness. *Clack.* Acknowledged to himself that he had avoided knowing too much about just where they had the boy. *Clack.* Fan jerked back, here's June Wolf again, looking all fierce and disappointed. *I didn't know,* he told her. Her paper eyes glowed, *Pisstail.*

Too old, said Emmanuel. *All you females. Just using us to build you a future...*

The eyes in the picture agreed with him. The eyes didn't care. *You're the father, the grandfather,* she murmured caressingly, *all the fathers...* The fan again, *clack.*

Here's Ms. Church going on: "There've been some incidents, fights. I'm not saying Akinde has been the instigator, but he's been...involved. They have a zero tolerance policy at the home and Akinde's been put on notice. Unfortunately, the next stop for him is a more controlled environment."

Emmanuel gripped his walking stick for comfort and put all the authority he could command into his voice. *Lord*, he was out of practice dealing with these kinda folks. Had to call on his father, 'cause he had nothing left of any authority himself, he was too ashamed—or too scared. He borrowed Redman's voice—*help me, Daddy*—and he told her, "That won't be necessary. I'll talk to the boy."

Amazed, Emmanuel heard the borrowed voice emerge without a sign of his fear. Like having Redman in the room with him. Ms. Church gave him an ambiguous look and went on without commenting, "Now Nicole is another story. Ordinarily we would make an effort to have her adopted, although she's a little old for optimal placement." (Too old at what, five? Emmanuel marveled.) "But in this case she doesn't seem to be integrating into her new family unit. The fostering family thought she was unsettled after Akinde's visits, so they recommended and we agreed to limit contact and when that didn't work, to terminate it, but the result hasn't been satisfactory. Unfortunately there have been some behavioral problems. The foster family has tried treating the bedwetting and tantrums medically, but they're feeling overwhelmed. Under the circumstances, adoption doesn't seem too likely, although they're very fond of her. We could try another foster home, but a lot of current thinking in the field supports the reunification of siblings where appropriate—that is you're committed to applying for kinship fostering?"

Emmanuel just sat there, marveling.

"Mr. King?"

"Yes, Ma'am, I would like to apply," he said. *Clack.* Here's June Wolf again—*Yes, Pisstail*—but this time lending him the full light of her greeny-grey-yellow eyes.

"Fine, we can get the forms done today and set you up for orientation and the home study."

"And how long is that gonna take?" he asked.

"Could be as long as seven months, but under the circumstances, since we may need an immediate placement for Akinde and Nicole..." Ms. Church let her uncompleted answer float in the air. Eyes averted, she turned briskly to her lopsided credenza and pulled forms and pamphlets from cubbyholes and slots, stacking them in a pile that Emmanuel hoped wasn't all for him. She went on talking over her shoulder, but Emmanuel let her voice fade while in his mind he carried on his conversation with June Wolf.

Here's Ms. Church filling his hands with the very pile he feared. Emmanuel folded it all and stuffed it into his breast pocket where it formed a bulky shield over his heart. He could feel the woman's eyes on him, weighing him, measuring him, and the language of her eyes was different from the things she said. Emmanuel looked back, replying to her in this other language. With his lips he said, "Goodbye, Ms. Church."

"Goodbye, Mr. King," she said with hers. Rusty little fan gave another squalling clack—*Lord, why don't she oil that thing*—and June Wolf growled him her goodbye...*uncle*...*father*...*grandfather*...in the language of the wolves.

Emmanuel hit the street gasping for air, then stood there, braced against his cane, wall to his back, gazing out over the scene like a king surveying a ruined but victorious country. The sellers of handbags and bootleg T-shirts gathered there eyed him, gauging the remote chance of a sale and choosing silence instead.

Emmanuel assessed the damages. The bad news: it was worse than he thought. Doctor visits twice a year. Seven-month home study. Akinde on the verge of getting jailed for being beaten up. Two blameless children separated and crying for each other. The good news: he was stronger than he remembered. He'd rediscovered an Emmanuel he thought he'd lost, the part Emma Lee used to call his "bad angel self." The rage that could set an unbreakable grip. Like in the war. Like on the job. Yeah, that Emmanuel. Like a wolf. That was why they had come to him, he thought. He snorted once or twice with bitter laughter, shortage of foster parents. Yeah. He wondered how they got anybody at all. The emerging women detoured around him respectfully, recognizing his righteous rage; it was theirs.

He went striding down the street like a younger man, swinging his cane like he didn't need it, grabbed an old bus and took a jolting ride back to his neighborhood behind a burly, sullen driver crouched over the wheel like he was driving a tank into battle. Next to him a lady in a fancy dress hat gobbled a smelly tuna fish sandwich as if she hadn't eaten in a week. She was dripping oil on the newspaper in her lap, Emmanuel glancing down, was unsurprised to see what might have been the picture of a wolf disappearing beneath the drippings. Lady said something, smiling with oil on her chin, but Emmanuel only gave her an absent smile, sat there with his mind alive, thinking like a good chess player, *uh-huh*, twenty moves on ahead.

He got off the bus, walked a block or two to Mac's Barbershop & Male Emporium. Two grown men passed him on scooters, nearly knocking him down, and Emmanuel snorted. At sixteen he'd been out at sea, in the Merchant Marine and earning a grown man's pay, doing a grown man's job.

Out in front of Mac's Willie's three-legged dog was enjoying a well-earned rest. Dog was off the clock, so Emmanuel leaned over and rubbed the white spot on his forehead between his eyes. "You a good player, better'n Willie," he told him. Dog's mouth hanging open and grinning above the kerchief Willie kept on him instead of a collar. Long time ago, Emmanuel decided it probably wasn't an accident color of that dog's bandana always matched Mister Till's show handkerchief or his tie, but he wasn't gonna have a conversation about it.

Looking in the dog's dark serious eyes, Emmanuel remembered dreamwalker wolf telling him, "There are wolves among you." Started thinking about his boy Jerome's little dog. Used to take the boy over to the cathedral at 156th, not their church, but Jerome had a friend took him once for the blessing of the animals and then he always wanted to go back, take his dog. Mister Pim in Jerome's lap, behaving himself as usual, Jerome all grown up in his last little suit—the one he never outgrew. Emmanuel wondering about the blessing, people bringing up their pets: dogs and cats, birds, snakes, turtles, lizards, goldfish in a bowl, one time a lady had a glass cage of butterflies. Emmanuel wondering if they hadn't got it all turnt around and the animals should be blessing us.

Then he remembered putting Mister Pim on the bus to North Carolina, sent him down there to be company for his father. Neither of them, him or Emma, wanted the dog around after Jerome died, Mister Pim crying and whimpering and carrying on. But what finally got to Emmanuel was the dog's undying hope. Mister Pim looking out the window for hours, hoping to spot Jerome on his way home. People thought they were crazy, spending good money send a dog on a trip. Put him out in the street or call the ASPCA. But that was Jerome's dog, dog was family, and if family was a burden, family was a gift.

Emmanuel sighed, straightened his back. So, here he was, a family man again. He had his look at freedom. More than most people ever got. And it was a whole world—the world next door. He'd never considered it. He'd only begun to explore it. And now he never would. For he clearly saw that if he took up the burden of these children, took up the burden of the family man, it would be for the last time. This time, the burden would outlast the bearer. He would die in harness. And while it didn't matter to anyone else, it mattered to him—losing this last chance. He wasn't given to weeping, but if he had been, now he would have wept.

Some would tell him, if and when he told the tale, that what he had won was worth what he'd lost. He'd done it before and would do it again and in time might not remember what he had wondered, here in this bittersweet hour.

Tilting his head, he could just see past the ancient, dusty jade plant—like a dwarfed, flat-leaved tree—occupying most of Mac's window. Willie G. was in the first chair with MacRae behind him shaving the point of his big chin, MacDaniel in the corner with a chessboard and a used-looking newspaper. Akinde over in the back, narrow shoulders bent over a push broom, sweeping up hair. Emmanuel gave Willie's three-legged dog a last chuck under his white spotted chin and went on in.

"Here he is! The Man of the Hour!" MacRae all excited for some reason, leaving Willie in the chair half-shaved to bustle over, wiping broad hands on his smock. Behind him, Akinde's face over his shoulder was thin and a little ashy. Had on a tight little expression Emmanuel finally allowed himself to recognize as fear. Then MacRae's broad body blocked his view of the boy.

"Brother Mariner! Come over here, somebody I want you to meet." MacRae seized his hands and almost dragged him over to a gentleman waiting his turn by the window. "Rev. Wolf, this here is Mr. Emmanuel King. Mr. King, meet Rev. Wolf. He's visiting from Atlantic City. Rev. Wolf, tell Mr. King what you tol' us."

"Nice to meet you, Reverend," said Emmanuel automatically, offering his hand. And then his attention, absent and intent on the boy, kicked in. *What* did MacRae say the man's name was?

The reverend looked up at him. Man had a mane of grizzled hair surrounding a dark-skinned face with serious eyes, dark-covered book in his hand, finger holding his place. Reverend started droning in a sonorous voice 'bout being ready to meet yo' creator at any time, at *all* times... "We're grass, Mr. King, we're leaves in th' wind." Emmanuel stood there confused, looking at MacRae beaming at him like it was his birthday while the stranger went on 'bout dying at short notice.

"MacRae. MacRae. Rae! Come back over here and finish wid me." Willie G. getting short-tempered with lather drying on his face. MacRae laughed like a loon and hurried back over to his chair, gave Wild Bill's face a few last swipes with the razor, still chuckling. Then the reverend started citing scripture and Emmanuel took a cautious few steps backward, never mind what the man's name was. Meanwhile, Akinde watching him all anxious, pretending to sweep.

MacRae slapped aftershave on Wild Bill. The smell, citrus, pine and musk oil, hung pungent in the air before it mingled with the other smells of the shop: MacDaniel's ginger beer, grilling meat from across the street, soap, old newspapers piled in the corner, dust, floor wax.

Willie stood up. "What he's talking about, Emmanuel, is that lawyer you hired for Barry finally kicked the bucket." Reverend Wolf frowned at this unseemly interruption. Willie grinned and went on, "Look like you won the bet."

Emmanuel had to sit down, strength gone out of his legs. He groped for a chair behind him, settled into it, tried to take a breath. Looked up to see Akinde hovering, asking him, "You okay, Granddaddy?"

It would only be a delay counted in minutes, and maybe it could have waited till he sorted through this other business, but the moments Akinde still wore that narrow-face look of fear now seemed very long to Emmanuel. He reached with a shaky hand into his breast pocket, half-pulled out the folded bundle of department paperwork and showed it to the boy for just a second, dark eyes riveted to light, and tucked it back. Watched as Akinde's face smoothed out like a newly made bed.

Emmanuel turned back to the stranger. "Rev. Wolf, I want to thank you for letting me know. Didn't really know the man, jus' had some business with him. He helped me out with a family matter. I'm truly sorry to hear about his passing. He a member of your congregation?"

"No," said the preacher. "I don't think he was a member of any Christian fellowship."

Willie snorted, "What he was was the sharpest practicin' attorney in Atlantic City, or leastways in Bungalow Park." Willie twisted around to glare up at MacRae behind him, still beaming while he brushed off Willie's broad shoulders; then Willie jerked himself around to address MacRae's partner MacDaniel, brooding over his chessboard in the corner. "See Rae?" Willie growled. "See Dan? I tol' you how he would be." MacRae favored him with his sunny smile. MacDaniel gave him a look of supreme indifference.

"If you mean I wouldn't be jumping up and down because a man is dead, yes, yes, you right, that is how I would be. Let me remind you," said Emmanuel, picking up the threads of that old, old argument with Willie, "He made the deal I asked him for."

William Tilly snorted at him, disgusted, glaring at him sideways. He peeled the wrapper from a cigar, stuck it in his mouth. "Yeah, I'm sure you thought up that pension givaway all by yo'self. Wonder how many other folkses' lives he had locked up in that filing cabinet of his." Muttered under his breath, "Bet they havin' themselves a party down in Bungalow Park." Emmanuel decided to ignore him. He had Akinde to think about, over there watching and listening wide-eyed, pretending to polish bottles with a rag.

Wild Willie stood up, settled his straw hat on his round head. Emmanuel noted with a certain mean satisfaction that today Willie's tie, show handkerchief *and* the band on his hat all matched the bandana on his three-legged dog. Then Willie G. gave him another sidelong look, turned his back, went over to glare at the street from the doorway, the set of his shoulders still tellin' Emmanuel how mad he was.

Reverend Wolf took a seat in the first chair and MacRae snapped a fresh bib in the air and settled it snug and snowy under the reverend's full salt and pepper beard. Bib one of them old-fashion touches kept Emmanuel coming in here, aside from the fact MacRae—MacDaniel too—was a brother Mariner. MacRae started snipping delicately at the reverend's grizzled mane. MacDaniel didn't even look up, must be one a' them days he felt too evil to work.

"I hope you won't have a legal battle on your hands, Mr. King? To reclaim your pension? Mr. MacRae has told me something of the circumstances." Something! Emmanuel snorted, look to him like MacRae put *all* his business on the street. But he didn't know everything. MacRae grinned down at him, sly, guilty and satisfied. "I had to tell him something, Mr. King, I just asked him to keep an eye on the situation for you."

"Legal battle," snorted Willie in the doorway without turning around. "All he hav' to do is stop sending them checks." Hitched his shoulders, tucked his folded chessboard under his arm, strode out the door and into the street like a man who made a good living in an air-conditioned office, not picking up change winning games in a pocket park. Wave hit Emmanuel then, 'cause Barry had that same world-go-to-hell stance and walk, had it even up in the jail.

Akinde looking at him all wide-eyed, stopped even pretending to work. Even the grown-ups looking impressed by this much foolishness. Emmanuel frowned. Who'd of thought, they could make a man ashamed of *keeping* his word? Act like a poor man couldn't afford a word of honor...

Anyway, Willie didn't know everything either. Stopped sending checks years ago, had that automatic deduction set up on his bank account. Have to go down there next Tuesday and cancel that unless he could do it over the phone. Emmanuel was surprised to feel a wave—this time of nostalgia—for his days in the poorhouse. Things were simpler—fewer choices.

Too much had happened today. Have to call that Ms. Church tomorrow, change the income declaration. Emmanuel settled into the second chair, waiting for MacDaniel to notice him. Didn't feel like waiting for MacRae, have him up there grinning behind his back. Kept lookin' at MacDaniel until he folded up his paper and took up a pair of clippers.

MacDaniel cut his hair in his customary silence. Third best chess player in the neighborhood, maybe fourth now if Emmanuel had to start counting that square head boy in the rotation.

Emmanuel looked around, frowned repressively at Rae, still over there grinning like Christmas. No way to act. Emmanuel closed his eyes, refused to look at him. Sat there feeling the tug of MacDaniel's comb at his scalp and considered the question of the reverend's name. This another one of what Emmanuel had come to think of as his visitations? Or jus' a coincidence? He gave it some thought. MacDaniel's big hands brushed the cut hair off his neck. He could hear traffic outside, jazz on the radio, Monk doing "Mysterioso."

"Yeah, we got us an author here, Reverend Wolf. Got my copy right here, signed: *Heroism of the Merchant Marine 1941-1946.*" MacRae pulled the slim volume from his shelves to display to the visitor while Emmanuel felt the familiar mixture of pleasure and embarrassment. MacDaniel tapped his shoulder to let him know he was done, took the bib off, snapped it in the air. Emmanuel stood up. MacRae turning pages in the little blue book for the reverend, Akinde looking over Rae's shoulder with a dust rag in hand, surprised expression on his face. Emmanuel smiled at the boy. Tickled him to surprise the young, they always think they got you all figured out.

"Rae, can I borrow Akinde a little early? Family business."

"Sure, sure, Mr. King, no problem. I'll see you tomorrow, Akinde." MacRae put *Heroism of the Merchant Marine* back on its shelf, tucking it in tenderly like a conscientious mother.

"Nice to meet you, Reverend Wolf," said Emmanuel. "Sorry it couldn't be under better circumstances." The man nodded back at him, sitting there with all the solidity of a mountain under a snow drift. Akinde hung his apron on a peg and held the door open for Emmanuel.

Two of them headed on home. Emmanuel looked at his boy, measured him with his eye. Be as tall as he is next summer. Last yellow daylight casting tall shadows in their paths. They passed a shop, Ruby's Robes, breathing gospel music into the open air. A block further on a shadowy form trotted across their paths, just a shepherd mix, with a little lab maybe, but the dog gave Emmanuel a start anyway. Dreamwalker's voice whispering in the back of his mind, *You have wolves among you.*

Akinde's face turnt round to his in the dusk. That narrow-face look gone. Boy's face smooth, trusting, blooming with that unconscious childish greed, greed that devours the parent, consumed for an unknown future. *Oh, yeah,* well, Emmanuel had seen that look before.

Okay, said Emmanuel to himself in the dusk, *okay. One last time.*

They passed the pocket park where Willie waved genially to them from his seat before the board, his three-legged dog at his feet. And then they took a shortcut through the playground. There, in the shadow of the buildings at dusk, a couple of kids were playing wheelchair basketball. Emmanuel and Akinde stood there wondering for a little while, and then they went in.

ABOUT THE AUTHORS

MARY WOLOS-FONTENO • *The Legend of Nookapingwa*
Mary Wolos-Fonteno is a freelance writer who lives in northern New Jersey with her husband, her daughter and their two cats. She's an animal lover who believes that animals lend balance to man's world and inner nature with their powerful spirits and presence.

While visiting New York City's Central Park Zoo on a hot summer day, Gus, the polar bear, supplied the inspiration for writing the "Legend of Nookapingwa" with his poolside antics and an empty barrel. This is her first published short story.

DEBBIE DIENEMAN • *Foxes of Fire and Ice*
Debbie Dieneman's love for animals has always been a major influence in her writing and her art. Her animal stories have appeared in children's magazines, including New York City Audubon Society's *Look Around New York*. Some of the children's books that she has illustrated include *The Good Morning Grump* (Abingdon Press), *Puss in Boots*, *The Easter Bunny*, *The Three Little Pigs*, and *Classic Poems for Children* (Andrews and MacMeel).

Dieneman is currently the Volunteer Coordinator for the Animal Department of the Prospect Park Zoo. She lives in Brooklyn, New York, with her husband Paul, daughter Kristen, three cats, and two turtles.

NANCY RAKOCZY • *Snake's Loose!*
Nancy Rakoczy is a poet and illustrator whose poems have appeared in *National Catholic Reporter*, *Perspectives* and *Olivetree Review*. Her illustrations have appeared in many publications and can most recently be seen in *Great Mystics and Social Justice* and other books published by Paulist Press. Rakoczy is currently a candidate for a Masters in Secondary Education English at Hunter College. She is a recipient of the Point of Purchase Advertising International (POPAI) award for design.

She presently lives in Queens, New York.

LINDAMICHELLEBARON • *The Lion and The Man*
Lindamichellebaron has entertained a lifelong love of Aesop's

fables. "The Lion and The Man: A Fable" is the second story in her fable series. Her first was the picture book, *Anthony Ant and Grady Grasshopper*. Lindamichellebaron has been publisher and president of Harlin Jacque Publications for over 20 years. Her poems are collected in *The Sun Is On, Rhythm & Dues*, and *For the Love of Life*. Her work has also appeared in several children's anthologies. Her most recent book, *No More Chocolate Chips!*, is published by renowned literacy advocate Wally Amos.

Lindamichellebaron has won numerous awards including the designation as Hempstead, New York's "Village Griot." She holds a doctorate in Cross Categorical Studies and is presently an assistant professor at York College, of the City University of New York (CUNY) in the Department of Teacher Education. You can find out more about Lindamichellebaron on her website www.lindamichellebaron.com.

M. KASKEL • *Percival Zeart*

"Percival Zeart" is M. Kaskel's first published writing. Kaskel believes all good gifts are from God and that it is never too late to use them, to look for them in others and to encourage their growth.

Kaskel encourages the adoption of shelter pets, especially the one with that quirky little difference.

CHEY BACKUSWALCOTT • *Okay Johnson*

Chey Backuswalcott has been an artist-in-residence at the Guggenheim and received Guggenheim Museum's Art Star for Children Award.

Chey Backuswalcott's artwork has been exhibited at galleries throughout the United States, and in Paris and London. Her artwork has been published in *The New York Times, Color To Color, New York Art Review, Essence*, and *Stanford Business* among other places. Her work is in many private collections, including those of Camille Cosby, Geoffrey Beene, Oprah Winfrey, Gertrude Crain, Jasmine Guy and Susan Taylor. She has fulfilled commissions for institutions such as Times Square, Barcardi, and the Alvin Ailey American Dance Theater.

Chey Backuswalcott has written several manuscripts for children and educators. "Okay Johnson" is her first published story.

MYRA NDANU CONSUELA • *Squirrel Paradise*

Myra Ndanu Consuela draws inspiration for her writing from her faith, her large, close family and rich colorful neighborhoods, including Harlem where she grew up and Flushing, NY where she has lived for 30 years. For 20 years she has been the publisher and editor of *Children's Focus*, a monthly newsletter about cultural activities available to families in New York City. Her forthcoming projects include *New York Celebrates*, a non-fiction book about special events and traditions in the city during the holidays.

Consuela is a founding member of Pen & Rose. "Squirrel Paradise" is her first published story.

VICTORIA JOHNSON • *Saving Kenya Kesi*

Victoria Johnson is a freelance writer who lives in Northern New Jersey with her husband, daughter and the various animals who enrich her life daily. In addition to being a writer, she is an interior designer, graphic designer and stained glass artist, as well as a jazz vocalist who teaches piano and voice.

Victoria is an avid reader and has a vested interest in the world of the past and the present. The background research for "Saving Kenya Kesi" fueled her interest and provided great insight into what is required to keep our animal heritage alive.

CHERYL HANNA • *Brother to the Wolf*

Cheryl Hanna is an artist, book designer and illustrator. She has illustrated several children's books including the award winning books *An Enchanted Hair Tale* and *Hard to Be Six*.

Hanna's collages and paintings have been widely exhibited in a number of venues including The Brooklyn Museum. Illustrations from her books, *An Enchanted Hair Tale* and *Stagecoach Mary Fields* have been exhibited at the National Museum of Women for the Arts and also forms part of the collection of the Mazza Museum, a museum dedicated to the art of children's book illustration, in Findley, Ohio.

Hanna is currently at work on a novel, *Tunisian Moon*, that is set in North Africa and combines her love of fairy tales, fascination with magic and the imagined lives of animals.

Hanna is a founding member of Pen & Rose. She lives in Brooklyn, New York. "Brother to the Wolf" is her first published story.

ACKNOWLEDGEMENTS

This book is dedicated to India DuBois, a writer of Pen & Rose who died too early to bring all her works to life. Author of the poetry collection, *Jazz in the Evening Sun*, it is perhaps her poetry developed in Pen & Rose about the vulnerable female spirit, that will ultimately bring us into her life and into our own lives.

India loved to write and did it almost daily. She'd call me all day long and read something to me. Or, she'd call and just laugh—it was infectious—and all you could do is laugh hysterically with her. After about an hour of this, she'd say, "I'll call you back later." Often, when she called back it was for another round of laughter.
—*Chey Backuswalcott for Pen & Rose*

Grateful appreciation is due to our editor, Kiini Ibura Salaam and to our copyeditors, Geoffrey Jacques and Tawanna Lambert for their careful reading of the manuscript and their countless helpful suggestions. Thanks are also due to Claire M. Wyckoff for additional editorial help and to Mrs. Ignatius Rakoczy for her generous support of this project.
—*The Writers of Pen & Rose*

Heartfelt appreciation is extended to Sandy Kennedy Bright for her unyielding commitment to sharing her strong belief in the value of folk tales and traditional storytelling. I commend her for the years of dedication and all the opportunities she has provided for the young storytellers of New York City. In addition, I especially thank Sandy for continually promoting ways and means for me to encourage the love of literature in children, families and educators.
—*Lindamichellebaron*

I would like to thank my fellow writers for their loving support and mostly gentle prodding.

Also a big thanks to an unknown keeper and tour guide at the Central Park Zoo for answering my questions about penguin zoo life. And thanks to Debbie for her tour of the Prospect Park Zoo, both

helped with getting a feel for the behind-the-scenes environment.
— M. Kaskel

The inspiration for "Okay Johnson" came from my art students at P.S. 19 in District 2M, in the East Village.

I'd like to thank Chris and Quentin, who insisted that all Pen & Rose Sunday meetings were to take precedence over their birthday parties and other family events.

Thank you to the real Das and Zorida whose names I used in the story.

And thank you to Lloyd and Doris Backus, principals and loving parents, who never abandoned me because my difference was creativity. Lastly, special thanks to my brothers, who supported my creativity blindly. They were always there for the next big project.

—Chey Backuswalcott

I thank my mother, Dorothy Matthews, and my son, Kenge Henry, for all their support and my grandnephews, Jamal, Isaiah, Emmanuel and Joshua for their inspiration.

—Myra Ndanu Consuela

I'd like to thank the writers of Pen & Rose for their patient listening, their helpful comments and (occasionally) warm cookies. I'd also like to thank my model, Mr. Leroy Henderson, for posing for Emmanuel.

—Cheryl Hanna

Printed in the United States
202170BV00002B/256-354/A